MUR
BOOKKEEPER'S ATTIC

DI MCKENZIE BOOK 3

ANNA-MARIE MORGAN

This book is dedicated to my grandmother, my mum's mum, whose given name was Rosemary Whitlock (1917-1977). We lost her to cancer in 1977, when I was 7 years old. I knew, for the first time, how devastating it feels to lose someone so precious.

What follows, is a work of fiction.

ALSO BY ANNA-MARIE MORGAN

The DI McKenzie Series (3 books so far)

Book 1 - Murder on Arthur's Seat

Book 2 - Murder at Greyfriars Kirk

Book 3 - Murder in the Bookkeeper's Attic

The DI Giles Series (22 books so far)

Book 1 - Death Master

Book 2 - You Will Die

Book 3 - Total Wipeout

Book 4 - Deep Cut

Book 5 - The Pusher

Book 6 - Gone

Book 7 - Bone Dancer

Book 8 - Blood Lost

Book 9 - Angel of Death

Book 10 - Death in the Air

Book 11 - Death in the Mist

Book 12 - Death under Hypnosis

Book 13 - Fatal Turn

Book 14 - The Edinburgh Murders

Book 15 - A Picture of Murder

Book 16 - The Wilderness Murders

Book 17 - The Bunker Murders

1

MURDER IN THE ATTIC

L achlan Campbell heard the clock in the hall strike midnight as he sat in the converted attic of his Edinburgh townhouse, surrounded by his precious collection of old and rare books. He read his journal entry one last time before putting down his pen and tidying papers under the amber glow of a Victorian bronze desk lamp. He rubbed the small of his back, blinking tired eyes, and gazed up at the moon through the skylight.

A creaking came from the stairs and he froze, hand poised over the lamp switch. Heart racing, he strained to hear through the thick veil of quiet that followed.

Nothing.

Perhaps his mind, addled with fatigue, was playing tricks. He switched off the light, dismissing the noise as the mere creaking of his old home.

A lone figure moved with lethal intent.

Before Lachlan sensed the danger behind, a garrotte came down around his neck, pulling taut with a violent jerk. Papers tumbled to the ground, and cascades of books toppled from *shelves as the desperate man clawed at the wire cutting into his flesh. It was a battle Lachlan's aging body would not win.*

The bookkeeper grew limp, slumping forward, his light extinguished among the scattered pages of a lifetime's work.

IN THE DREICH OF A DAMP, Scottish spring morning, Grant locked the car, knowing his colleagues would be on scene already. He checked his watch and grimaced. The school run had set him back a good half-hour.

A woman in her thirties waited on the doorstep of the Edinburgh townhouse, dressed in a tracksuit and apron. A loose ponytail held brunette hair off her shocked, ashen face, and her lower lip trembled as she spoke. "Inspector McKenzie?" she asked.

"Aye, that's me." He nodded.

"He's up there." She pointed to a window high above the street. "I've never seen anything like it. That poor man. What he must have gone through..." The words poured out of her like milk from a carton with too large an opening, stumbling over each other in their race to be told.

Grant's blue eyes scanned her face.

"Sheila Fletcher," she added. "I'm Lachlan's cleaner. Was... Was his cleaner. I found him this morning. Had the shock of my life." Her hand shook as she pushed stray hair from her face, eyes round.

"When did you last talk to him?" McKenzie looked beyond her, at the PC on the door, pressing his lips into a thin line as he watched uniformed officers cordon off the house with tape; blocking the road to prevent contamination and onlookers disturbing the scene.

"Yesterday afternoon," she replied, pushing her hands

into the apron's pockets. "He was talking about this new book he got a hold of... Said it was priceless, so he did. I've never seen him so excited."

"Really?" The DI made notes. "Do you know what it was called, this book?"

She shook her head. "I don't, I'm sorry. He might well have told me, but it went in one ear and out the other. I mean, he was always talking about some old book or other and, well... that was his passion. It wasn't mine." She looked down at her shoes. "I feel bad now. I should have paid better attention."

"Aye well... Hindsight is a wonderful thing." Mckenzie snapped his notebook shut. "We'll need a full statement from you, Mrs Fletcher. But right now, take a moment... You've had quite the shock. Someone will be with you shortly. I'd advise you to sit down with a cuppa till then."

He climbed the narrow stairs to Lachlan Campbell's attic. A lone skylight lit the gut-wrenching scene within, and the air was heavy with the scent of old books and the metallic tang of blood.

"Grant," DC Graham Dalgleish greeted him with a nod, tie loose; top button undone. "It's pretty grim. He must have put up one hell of a fight."

McKenzie cast his eyes over the scene. "Killer must have been strong."

Lachlan's body lay slumped over the desk, face turned to the side, shock and pain evidenced by his open mouth and frozen stare. Papers and books lay strewn across the floor and the bookkeeper's desk, the chaotic mess a silent testament to the struggle which ended the bibliophile's life.

"Where's forensics?" McKenzie glanced at his watch. "They should have been here by now."

"They're on their way." Dalgleish shrugged. "Probably caught in traffic."

DS Susan Robertson snapped on a pair of latex gloves, her gaze not leaving the body. Kneeling beside the victim, she examined him for signs of trauma other than the obvious ligature marks around his neck. "Garrotted," she confirmed tersely, looking up at McKenzie, "Poor bugger... Have you seen this scratched next to him?" She moved over, allowing the DI and Dalgleish to see.

Beside the body, etched into the wooden floorboards, was a circle, roughly ten centimetres in diameter, containing letters the letter 'T' and 'K', and symbols that included an open book, and an owl.

Grant knelt to examine it. "Photograph this," he instructed the plastic-suited photographer, as soon as he entered the door. "I want high-resolution images, from different angles. We'll run it through the database, see if it matches anything we've seen before."

"Well-spotted, Sue." The DI snapped the carving on his mobile. "It could be the killer's signature. Have you seen anything else?" He asked, offering the DS a hand up.

"Not anything like that," Susan replied, knees clicking as she rose. "But I'll bet my boots this wasn't a random break-in. It looks targetted to me."

"Aye." McKenzie nodded, pondering the enigmatic symbol. Was it a message from the killer? A sign recognisable only to the initiated? Or a red herring meant to send them down blind alleys? "Let me know the results from the database," he said, his brow furrowed. "Let's hope you're right, and this isn't a crazed serial killer, offing random strangers."

Dalgleish examined the bookcases, gingerly stepping over contents now lying on the floor. "This collection was his pride and joy. It's a damn shame," he murmured, picking up a leather-bound volume from the floor with gloved hands. His fingertips traced the embossed spine before he placed it back where he got it from.

McKenzie examined the layout of the room. "Campbell had his back to the attacker. Whoever did this took him by surprise."

"Aye," Dalgleish responded. "The killer likely knew the house, and Lachlan. I don't believe this was random. There was no forced entry."

"How did the attacker gain access?" The DI frowned.

"We found the backdoor unlocked. My best guess is the killer came in that way."

"The victim told the cleaner about a rare book he had come by. He was really excited about it. That was yesterday afternoon, only hours before his murder."

"Does she know which book? Or what it looked like? We ought to know if it is still here, or if the killer took it. The killer left such a mess. It's hard to know whether anything is missing."

"Unfortunately not. She didn't pay him much heed. Her mind was on the cleaning."

SCENE OF CRIME officers arrived and began collecting samples, dusting for fingerprints, and testing for blood. They placed each seized item in a plastic bag, tagging them for evidence.

Dr Fiona Campbell, the pathologist, joined them, carrying her leather case.

"Hey..." Grant greeted her. "The victim is no relation, is he?"

She answered him with a mock stern look. "Ach, there's nay just one Campbell family in Edinburgh, McKenzie."

He grinned. "Aye, I ken, but I thought I'd better check."

She tossed her head, smiling despite herself, before kneeling near the victim, and speaking into a dictaphone, her expression grave. "Garrotted... The weapon was a metal wire with wooden handles. The broken flesh still contains the embedded line. The wound was so deep it bled down the neck. Make sure you bag those hands," Fiona instructed the nearest forensic officer. "The victim struggled with his attacker. There may be skin under the fingernails."

Grant pulled a face. "Judging by the scratches around the garrotte, I'd say most of that skin will be the victim's own."

"Sure..." She nodded. "But we can extract his profile from anything we get. Whatever is left over will probably be the killer's."

The DI nodded. "Fingers crossed..."

"Careful with those," DS Robertson advised DC McAllister, gesturing toward the books strewn around the floor. "I don't think the photographer has finished yet."

"Aye, I've got it," Helen assured her, teetering around the perimeter of an attic now cramped with police and forensic personnel. A space originally designed as Lachlan's private sanctuary was all but overrun, as they scoured it for evidence.

McKenzie left them to it, deciding to rejoin the cleaner, Sheila Fletcher, while her memories were still fresh.

He found her in the galley kitchen, sat at the wooden table with a cup of tea, accompanied by a female officer in uniform. The scent of antiseptic wafted on the air, replacing the odour of death in the DI's nostrils. "Mrs Fletcher," he began, voice soothing as he pulled out a chair opposite. "I need you to tell me everything you remember about last night and this morning. Are you able to talk now?"

"Aye." She nodded, hands clasped tight around her mug; eyes glazed.

"When did you last see Mr Campbell alive?"

She put the vessel down, wringing her hands; eyes darting toward the ceiling, as though seeing him in the attic above. "It was late afternoon when I left. I went upstairs to tell him I was going. And he was up there, in his attic, surrounded by his books and papers as usual."

"I thought you last spoke to him earlier in the afternoon?"

"Aye, that was when we had our last conversation. He didn't answer when I said goodbye. I don't think he heard me. He was far too engrossed in what he was writing. Lachlan had this big book open and was making notes from it. I assumed it was the really rare book he had told me about. He seemed lost in it, anyway, and was muttering to himself as he scribbled away. He didn't look up."

"Could you make out what he was saying?"

"No, I couldn't. Lachlan had his back to me and was bent over his desk. He was speaking too quietly for me to make out the words. I decided against disturbing him when he was so deep in thought. I left the house without a further word."

"What time would that have been?"

"Och... Around four-ish, I would say. I caught the four-fifteen bus, and was home by five."

"Did you notice anything unusual? Any unexpected visitors or perhaps something out of place?" McKenzie pressed, intense gaze missing nothing.

"Not ...really, just..." Sheila Fletcher hesitated, shaking her head as though fighting with the images in her mind.

"There was a car I didn't recognise parked on the street when I arrived. But it was gone when I left, and I thought little of it."

"Can you describe the car?" McKenzie made a note.

"It was a light in colour... white, or silver maybe? Could have been a BMW, but I'm not great with cars, so I canna be sure." she admitted, her voice faltering. "I don't know much about vehicles because I don't drive myself. I've never needed to in Edinburgh. Me and my husband... well, we don't have kids. My husband drives for work and takes me places, and I get the bus to and from work. I always have."

"Can you recall what Mr Campbell said to you about the rare book? Was it a first edition? Did he buy it? Or did someone give it to him?"

She shook her head, pulling a face. "I don't know, I'm sorry. But he was active on social media," she added quickly. "He sometimes put things on his profile. He was a widower... Lost his wife in his sixties. But he has grown children and grandchildren. I don't think he saw much of them, but he kept in touch on Facebook. You might want to start there. He friended me ages back, so I have the link to his profile if you need it."

"Thank you, Mrs Fletcher. That would be helpful. And we can check CCTV for the car you mentioned, but we'll need a detailed statement from you for our records, covering everything you have told me today, if that's okay?"

"Aye, no problem," she answered, her eyes glazed over once more.

McKenzie offered her a reassuring smile, his mind mulling over what she'd said. He stood, asking the female officer if she would kindly assist Sheila Fletcher with her statement, as he turned for the door.

"The Whitlock Tome," Sheila declared. "That was it. He

said it was The Whitlock Tome." She lifted round eyes to the DI. "I just remembered."

Grant scribbled the name in his notebook. "Thank you, Mrs Fletcher."

AS HIS TEAM left the victim's home to return to Leith station, the Grant focussed on their next moves. "I want us checking CCTV, dashcam footage, and Lachlan Campbell's social media accounts. Talk to the family and neighbours; maybe someone saw or heard something. And, finally, I want every database checked for the insignia scratched on the floor. If the killer left it, we want to know why. Meanwhile, we need to find out everything we can about the Whitlock Tome."

The DI stayed back for a moment, surveying the house from the street. The unassuming frontage belied the horror within its walls. But someone else had stood on that same street. Someone with evil intent. A killer staring up at the house from the darkness, planning their attack before entering and creeping upstairs to the moonlit attic. The DI pushed clenched hands deep into his pockets. "We'll get you," he said out loud. "Whatever it takes."

2

THE WHITLOCK TOME

G raham Dalgleish tapped his keyboard, flicking through dozens of images and articles, oblivious to his colleagues in Leith Police Station, as he researched Lachlan's late acquisition. According to Wikipedia, the famous English writer Rosemary Whitlock completed the Whitlock Tome while her husband was fighting in France in the First World War. It became famous after going missing in the late nineteen-twenties. Supposedly, the book contained the secrets to a family fortune, and collectors worldwide had been searching for it ever since it disappeared. Had their victim really found this book? And was this the motive for his murder?

The DC waded through Lachlan Campbell's life as it unfurled through social media posts, snippets of text, images of well-worn books, and comments from fellow bibliophiles. "Come on, Lachlan, help us find your killer," he muttered, scrolling past pictures of filled libraries and quaint reading nooks. "Did you photograph the book?"

He was about to stop and rest his eyes when a post dated three weeks prior grabbed his attention. It was a photo of a dusty, leather-bound volume resting atop an old oak desk, similar to a dozen others he had come across in his search. But the caption underneath sent his pulse racing. He leaned closer, squinting as he read the elegant word emblazoned on the book's spine. It had to be the one, but it surprised him that 'Tome' was not in the title at all. Only one word — Rosemary's surname, Whitlock.

"Grant?" he called, slicing through the office chatter, focus still on the post in which Lachlan Campbell claimed to have stumbled upon a literary Holy Grail. "Sir, come and take a gander at this."

McKenzie strode to Dalgleish, his tall frame casting a shadow over the DC's desk as he leaned over his shoulder. "What have you found?"

"Take a look..." Graham pointed at the screen. "Lachlan's social media post three weeks before he died. He's talking about the book, referring to it as the Whitlock Tome, and stating the author wrote it during The Great War. But the book's title is only one word — Whitlock. You can see it on the spine. Wikipedia stated Rosemary wrote it during The Great War. This has to be the one."

The DI leaned in closer, narrowed eyes scanning the text, hand pushed into the pockets of his trousers as read the post. "The Whitlock Tome... That's it. That must be the book Sheila Fletcher was referring to." He began reading. "Penned between 1914 and 1918 by Rosemary Whitlock while her husband fought in France."

"Aye, and if Lachlan really had this book, we may have found ourselves the motive for his murder." Graham leaned back in his chair, chest puffed out.

"Wait, though..." Grant frowned. "We've been in his home, and in his attic. The desk in this photo is not his. And that's not his house." Grant straightened up. "Perhaps it's a photo of the place he got the book from? If so, then the owner of that desk might tell us more. Keep digging, Graham. try to find out where that photo came from, and anything else you can about that book."

"Aye, all right. But I'll have myself a brew first, eh?"

The DI grinned. "Only if you make one for everyone."

"Jings… You drive a hard bargain, you." Dalgleish tossed his head, tutting loudly. "I'm just the office slave."

AN HOUR LATER, and Dalgleish remained engrossed in the search; every ounce of focus on his screen.

"Any luck?" McKenzie perched on the edge of his desk.

"Bits and bobs…" Dalgleish looked up from an old auction listing he was going through. "It's like chasing a wraith through the mist. I'll let you know as soon as I have something concrete."

"Keep at it. We need to know if Lachlan really got a hold of that book and, if so, where he got it from. Sheila Fletcher, his cleaner, said he told her he had possession of it. But she also said he would have posted confirmation on his social media to say so. And it doesn't look like he did that exactly. His post is enigmatic, to say the least."

"Aye, he describes it, and shows that photo, but doesn't say it is his." Graham shook his head. "Maybe we should ask the cleaner again. She could have gotten mixed up."

"Aye well, if we don't find what we need today, I'll go back to her; find out how sure she is of what he said."

MEANWHILE, Helen McAllister approached the DI with more bad news.

"I'm sorry, Grant, but they've not found the killer's DNA. Only Lachlan's own DNA was under his fingernails. There were no prints, and no DNA traces on the garrotte, and no shoe prints anywhere inside or outside of the property. CCTV from the street has yielded nothing for the hours around the murder, but there are no cameras at the back of the houses. We don't have footage of a light-coloured BMW."

"Oh, hell..." McKenzie ran a hand through his hair.

"But we have fibres... Black wool, possibly from gloves, recovered from the wound in Lachlan's neck. They were under the wire as it dug into his flesh."

"Well, that's something, at least."

"Sir," Dalgleish called out to the DI, who was reading the forensic results. "This book has one of the most fascinating histories I've read. No wonder people have been searching for it for so long. It's mostly rumour, unfortunately, but the details check out."

"Fascinating how?" McKenzie folded his arms, leaning back as Dalgleish approached his desk.

"Get this..." Graham read from his notes. "I looked up Rosemary's publisher, and they make no reference to the book. It is neither listed, nor does it have an ISBN registered anywhere in British records. So I researched Yorkshire records for information about the family and discovered they had some wealth, and a mansion handed down through the male Whitlock line."

"Go on..."

"The Whitlocks had been staunch royalists, fighting with Cavaliers against the Roundheads."

"Okay... And how does that fit in?"

"It doesn't... It's just an interesting fact." Graham pulled a face. "Right, getting back to the book... Historical records for the house and the Whitlock family refer to Rosemary's book, stating she wrote it for posterity. Her husband, David, was the last of the Whitlock male line, and she was terrified of him being killed in battle. She wanted to ensure his legacy and history would live on if he didn't return from France." Dalgleish paused. "I should also say the Records do not confirm the book's existence. They only state *that* they believed Rosemary wrote it when David Whitlock left for France in nineteen-fourteen. But the fact they mention it in their records in an entry from nineteen-thirty is a good indicator of its existence, right enough."

McKenzie nodded. "It certainly appears to have existed."

"But..." The DC scratched his head. "They also say the book went missing when Rosemary died in the late nineteen-twenties. No-one knows exactly when it was stolen from the Whitlock family reading room, but it was sometime around nineteen-twenty-nine. The theft coincided with a bunch of rumours that were circulating, stating the book had encoded within it a secret related to the family fortune or the whereabouts of a priceless family heirloom." He shrugged. "So, it vanished in the twenties, only to resurface in whispers among collectors and bibliophiles a few months ago. Online talk suggested it was cursed, likely because of the Whitlock family's history of military men killed in battle or missing in action. David Whitlock, himself, was listed as missing in action, believed killed. His body, like so many others in battles around France, was never found. Other rumours say the book is a treasure map in disguise. No-one living can claim to have seen the thing in the flesh, but the legend is very much alive."

McKenzie pressed his lips together, forehead furrowed.

"So, regardless of whether the book actually existed, it could still be the killer's motive for murder."

"Team huddle. McKenzie's orders." Graham grinned, downing the dregs of his coffee.

The click of keyboards and conversations dwindled as they gathered their notepads and pens.

"Thank you for joining me at short notice," McKenzie began, his gaze sweeping the faces in front of him. "Graham's been researching the Whitlock Tome, the book Sheila Fletcher thinks Lachlan mentioned to her before his death. Sheila is sure he told her he had gotten hold of it and says he was writing copious notes on it." The DI cast his gaze around. "It seems every man and his dog have mentioned it over the years. But does it really exist? And, if so, where is it now? If the cleaner was right, and her employer had it, we have to assume the killer took it when he murdered him. We find the book; maybe we find Lachlan's killer. What I want to know is, if our victim got the book, where did he get it from? Was it paid for? Was it given to him? If he bought it, was it a private sale or a public auction? Where are such old books bought and sold? These are the questions for which we need urgent answers. Perhaps auction houses can tell us about individuals who were desperate to get their hands on this book. They may have names for us. Perhaps one name will stand out? In the meantime, we have Lachlan's friends, family, and acquaintances to interview. Perhaps they can may can shed light on who killed our victim and why."

Murmurs rippled through the room.

"Make no mistake," Grant continued, his tone serious. "This is no fanciful treasure hunt. Tread carefully. This killer is not afraid to use extreme violence. Perhaps Rosemary Whitlock encoded a family treasure within that book, or maybe the work is simply the historical record it purports to be. Whichever the case, we should investigate the book's origins and whereabouts. Our goal is to find out whether this book bears any relevance to Lachlan Campbell's murder."

"Online databases and archives might have something on Rosemary Whitlock," Helen offered. "I'll start with national records, and branch out to university collections and local repositories. If there's any trace of her tome or its history, I'll find it."

DS Susan Robertson cleared her throat. "Local historians might have something to offer too, especially for one of Edinburgh's own. Rosemary's maiden name was Wallace, and she grew up here. I'll reach out, see if they've heard whispers of the Whitlock family or the book."

"Good thinking, Sue," McKenzie nodded. "Let me know how that goes. Remember, time is against us. As will be the killer, if he thinks we're onto him. Any information released to the public must go through myself and the DCI. Any questions?"

Heads shook around the room.

"Okay then, let's get to work."

MCKENZIE STARED through the office window, thoughts whirling around like a winter gale off the Firth of Forth. He reached for the social media post Dalgleish had left on his desk. As his fingers traced the words, he pondered how Rosemary Whitlock's legacy and literary prowess had ended up overshadowed by this one elusive work. Had she an inkling of the book's power when she wrote it? Was it a last gift to her lost husband? Perhaps it was her way of insuring his name would live on despite having no male heir?

He thought of Sheila Fletcher. Was her flaky memory the result of discovering her employer's body? Or deliberate obfuscation?

He made a silent vow to a city that depended on them to keep its streets safe from predators. They would find and bring Lachlan Campbell's killer to justice. He would make sure of it.

3

FRIENDS OR FRENEMIES?

Wind howled through the narrow streets of Edinburgh, picking up the odd crisp packet and other discarded debris and whipping them around like bullets, as Grant approached the stone-clad dwelling belonging to Lachlan Campbell's friend, Douglas Stewart. The house, nestled within the heart of the city's historic district, loomed silent and brooding under a slate-grey sky. DI McKenzie paused, a taking a deep breath of the chill spring air before knocking the door.

A man in his late sixties with trembling hands opened it a minute later. His red-rimmed eyes blinked in the sunlight. "Inspector McKenzie?" he asked, voice cracking.

"Yes." The DI inclined his head. "Mr Stewart?"

"Come in." The older gentleman held the door for Grant to enter the foyer, a dimly lit area thick with the silence of tragedy. A clock chimed somewhere at the back of the house.

"Call me Douglas," the friend replied, gesturing toward the nearest doorway.

The room had a sombre ambience. Closed curtains and

a flickering firelight emphasised its shadows. The air smelled of aged paper and the stale stench of unfinished whisky which lay in a glass on a side table.

"Thank you, Douglas," McKenzie said, taking a seat across from him on a vintage leather sofa. "I am deeply sorry for your loss." He meant it.

Lachlan's friend nodded, clasping and unclasping his hands as though searching for something solid to hold on to. "He was like a brother to me. We'd known each other since we were just wee bairns."

"Can you tell me about him? His interests? His concerns? Anything that might help us understand what led to this terrible tragedy?" The DI's blue eyes searched the older man's face.

"He loved books," Douglas' gaze drifted towards towering bookshelves lining the walls. "Old books and rare editions. They were Lachlan's lifeblood." A wistful smile touched his lips, but quickly faded. "He'd been ecstatic these past weeks. Said he was finally getting his hands on something special. Said it was the Whitlock Tome."

"He told you that?" The DI's brows raised. "He was going to have the book written by Rosemary Whitlock?"

"Aye." Douglas nodded.

"Did you see it yourself at any point?"

He shook his head. "No, but he would have shown it to me if he'd lived." He sighed. "I think he may have had the book only a day or two before... Well, you ken..."

"Did he tell you why it was so important to him?"

"Only that it was rare. Valuable." Douglas looked away, lost in thought. "He mentioned something about a hidden message within its pages, but I never paid much heed to it. I mean, it wouldn't be the first time folks made such claims about old things. I remember the craze of playing vinyls backwards because people thought reversing the words revealed secret messages."

"Like Beatles' songs..." McKenzie grinned.

"Aye, exactly." Douglas shook his head. "I mean, the book's story intrigued me, right enough, but I doubted the rumours of hidden treasure were true. I told Lachlan as much. Told him not to get his hopes up."

"How did he respond?"

"He muttered something about it being more important than that." The man shrugged. "I don't know what he meant, and he didn't tell me."

"Did you ask him?"

Douglas's eyes shot to the DI's face. "Was it the book that got him killed?"

"We are keeping an open mind as to the killer's motives." McKenzie glanced at his notes. "When did you last see Lachlan?"

"Last Wednesday." Douglas turned his face towards the fireplace. "Six days ago."

"So, two days before his murder?"

"Aye, about that."

"And this is around the time you think he got the book?"

"He came to see me in the morning... If I remember rightly, he told me he had the book already. I don't know when exactly he received it. And I never saw him again."

"Did he say where he got the book from?"

"No."

"Did he tell you how the book arrived? Was it a van delivery? Postal? In person? Did he collect it?"

"He didn't say." Douglas shook his head. "I don't think there is anything more I can tell you about it, honestly, or about what happened to Lachlan. But I miss him popping by and talking about his books. I used to run a bookstore close to here. I retired five years ago. My back wasn't up to carrying them and climbing the ladders any more. Lachlan was my only connection to the trade now. I don't think he would ever have stopped collecting. That's the man he was. I enjoy books, but I didn't love them the way he did. Nor did I have the extensive knowledge he had of rare editions." He shrugged. "I think I've told you all I know."

McKenzie's mind picked over fragments of information as he watched Lachlan's friend, noting the tremble in his voice; the haunted look in his eyes. As he rose to leave, the DI knew only one thing for sure — this mystery was far from ordinary.

GRANT PULLED his coat tight against a chill wind as he approached the stone facade of Alistair MacGregor's Georgian townhouse. Tall sash windows gleamed from their sunlit position as the DI lifted the polished brass knocker and let it fall. The closing door echoed down the hallway as MacGregor ushered him into a world full of artefacts and amber.

"Thank you for seeing me," McKenzie said, taking it all in.

Dark wood panelling lined the hall, and an antique grandfather clock ticked methodically, its pendulum rhythmically marking time. Large glass cases dotted here and there displayed antiquities, both organic and man-made, all precisely annotated, many with brass tags.

"No problem, Inspector. In times like these..." MacGregor's voice trailed off, his expression solemn. Shadows lurking beneath his eyes suggested a restless night for the man, who appeared impeccably dressed in trousers, waistcoat, and tie.

"May I?" McKenzie gestured towards a sitting room to the left, where volumes of books lay scattered on mahogany surfaces, spines cracked from age and use.

"Aye, certainly," the man replied, leading the way.

They settled into vintage cloth armchairs that creaked under their weight.

McKenzie noted the faint scent of pipe tobacco. "I believe you and Mr Campbell shared an interest in antiques?" He began, watching the other man closely.

"Aye, indeed. He had an eye for a rare find. Mostly books, ye ken. Whereas I prefer objects, myself. But Lachlan had set his heart on one thing above all else. The Whitlock book."

"Would you describe him as obsessed with it?"

MacGregor stared ahead, as though seeing his dead friend again. "Consumed by it, I'd say. He'd been making notes... Lots of cryptic scribbles. Said they were essential to unlocking something big."

"Did you witness him writing these notes?" McKenzie cocked his head, eyes studying the other man's face. "We didn't find any such writings at his house. Nor did we find the book."

"Really?" MacGregor's eyes narrowed as he looked off into the distance. "Well now, that's a queer thing."

Grant frowned. What was the man thinking about? He cleared his throat. "The absence of this book, which you and others are sure should have been there, makes me suspect the killer took it... Someone wanted the Whitlock Tome enough to murder Lachlan for it. And you say there should have been notes with it, too. This agrees with what his cleaner said."

"Do you think the killer stole them and the book?"

"That might be the logical conclusion, don't you think?" The DI paused. "Unless you think Lachlan made it all up?"

"But why would he do that? Why act like he had the book of he didn't? That makes no sense."

McKenzie shrugged. "I'm only asking, because we found no proof he had it." He kept his tone even, his eyes staying on MacGregor's face.

"I wouldn't know…"

"But you say you saw him write the notes?" the DI pressed.

"The pages were on his table the last time I went to his house."

"Which was when?"

"Oh, I dunno… ten days ago, maybe?"

"How do you know they related to the Whitlock book?"

"He told me they did."

"Did he let you read them?"

"He handed them to me."

"What did they say?"

"Honestly? I don't remember verbatim. To be honest, my head was full of a delivery I was waiting for, and I confess to only humouring Lachlan because he was so excited. I could see it energised him, but I didn't have the same level of interest in it. I scanned the words over so he wouldn't feel disappointed. They made little sense to me. Perhaps I read them too quickly. I handed the pages back without really taking anything in. He had written them at speed, and deciphering the scrawl would have taken more time and energy than I had. You must remember, Lachlan had been researching both the book and the family. He knew the background, which was why it would all make sense to him, but it didn't to me. He forgot that in his excitement."

"Can you remember anything at all about them?"

"There was something in there about signed documents and meetings. It had something to do with David Whitlock, Rosemary Whitlock's lost husband. Honestly, I cannot remember more than that. Like I say, I really did not pay enough attention. I wish I had, right enough."

"Is there anything else you would like to tell me about Lachlan? Do you know anything about his murder?"

"Lachlan was a good man, an avid book collector, and a loyal friend. He didn't deserve what happened to him. My best guess is some other collector wanted that book and saw my friend as the barrier to getting it. He would never have sold it, you see. For Lachlan, the Whitlock book was a keeper. He wasn't looking at it as an investment. He was genuinely interested and enthralled by it."

"Thank you for your time." Mckenzie passed him a card. "Call us if you hear anything else you think we should know."

"I will. Anything to help bring Lachlan justice." The man shook the DI's hand with a firm grip.

As McKenzie stepped out into a now warmer Edinburgh day, his thoughts churned. Lachlan's murder appeared intimately connected with the Whitlock book, and maybe the bookkeeper's cryptic notes revealed why. Perhaps, if they could find them, his scribbles would lead to the killer.

Grant pushed open the weathered door of Canny Man's, a family-run bar and restaurant in Morningside, where

Lachlan had indulged in the occasional seafood meal and a Bloody Mary, for which the Canny Man's was famous. He passed a myriad of items hanging from the walls and ceilings, including an old typewriter, trumpet, and violin case.

His eyes rested on a lonely figure tucked away in a shadowy alcove, the avid geocacher he was here to meet.

The man looked up, gaze darting about the room as he chewed a thumbnail. He gave a shy nod. "DI McKenzie?" he asked, clearing his throat, about to stand.

The DI held up a hand. "Fergus Murray?"

The man nodded.

"Stay there, I'll join you." Grant slid into the seat opposite.

Murray was wiry, with hair the colour of Crammond sand. He sat hunched, long fingers picking at the beer mat under his half-emptied pint. He took a sip from the latter; the froth giving him a thin moustache before he licked it off. "I heard about Lachlan. It's such a shame... I can't believe it, actually." He studied Grant's face, as though gauging the detective's thoughts.

McKenzie nodded, seeing in Murray's expression a mixture of sadness and something else, harder to place. "I hear he sometimes went geocaching with you. Spent many weekends outdoors, I understand?"

"Aye, Lachlan had a love for it, especially if the prize was an old book. He was always chattering about some rare find or other."

"Did he include the Whitlock book in these chats?" Grant inclined his head, attempting to see beneath Murray's half-closed lids.

"Och, the Whitlock Tome..." Murray trailed off, shaking his head as if to dispel a troubling thought. "That was his white whale."

"You mean it was something he wanted but would never get?"

"Aye, that."

"But he got it, didn't he? Before he was murdered?"

Murray shrugged. "Says who?"

"Says several people who knew him..." McKenzie pressed his lips together.

"Did they see it themselves? The book, I mean?"

"Well, no..."

"Right."

"But they tell me Lachlan told them he finally had it."

"Interesting..." Murray scratched his head, angular face serious. "Maybe he found it then, or maybe he was looking for a reaction. He'd been searching for it a long time. Most of his friends and acquaintances were sceptical of the book's existence. You know that, right?"

"But Yorkshire records mention it."

"Aye, but has anyone ever really seen it?"

"Its writer was famous."

"Aye, exactly. If she said she wrote it, then people would believe her, right?"

"Are you saying she never even wrote the book?"

"I'm saying I have never seen proof she did. Nor has anyone else I have ever spoken to about it."

"You searched for it yourself, then?"

"Aye, I spent two years trying to track it down... Unbeknown to Lachlan, of course. I wanted to surprise him with it. Not that I could have afforded it if I found it, but at least I could have told him where it was."

"But you didn't find it?"

"Well, no... obviously. And, more to the point, I couldn't find evidence of it ever existing. Only references in archives to Rosemary Whitlock having written it, alleging she had hung on to the only copy during her lifetime."

"I thought it went missing in the nineteen-twenties?"

"Aye, it did... When Rosemary Whitlock died in nine-teen-twenty-nine. They say she never recovered from losing her husband. They say she died of a broken heart. Pined away, so to speak."

"I see."

"No-one has seen the book since. I couldn't find anyone who claimed to have seen it at all. Only those who repeat that it held hidden information said to be worth a fortune. People have been searching for it for nigh-on a century."

"What about Lachlan? What did he tell you about the book? Did he mention specific details? Taking notes? Or anything that might relate to his coming into possession of the book?" McKenzie watched the geocacher's reaction closely.

Murray's brow creased, a frown forming on his lips as he set the pint down. "No, I only know that Rosemary allegedly said the book held the key to a fortune, or words to that effect," Murray replied. "Well, you could read that any which way, even if it were true. If Lachlan was writing notes, they likely connected to Rosemary Whitlock's meaning when she said that. I'm not saying the Whitlocks were not wealthy, they were... But only as much as their friends. If what they say is true, perhaps Rosemary wanted their money to go to someone worthy, as she and her husband had no heir of their own."

"They were childless, then?"

"They were. David was in his mid-twenties when he went missing in action; presumed dead. And Rosemary never remarried."

"Did they not have other family?"

Murray shook his head. "David was an only child whose father had also died in combat. His mother remarried. She had inherited a proportion of the father's wealth, as did David, and she never sought more. People said that Rosemary had a falling out with her Scottish family, the Wallaces, when she married. They did not want her marrying into the English military, even mildly aristocratic military. They believed that way lay heartache. She never truly forgave them."

"Where is their money now?"

Murray shrugged. "That's anyone's guess. You could look into it. What's left of it is probably in some Swiss bank account somewhere."

"Is there anything else you can tell me about Lachlan?"

"Only that he was a good man, and I cared about him. Everyone did. He was genuine, and warm, with a good sense of humour."

"When did you last see him?"

"A couple of weeks back. We met here, actually. For a bite to eat, a pint, and a blether. He was in good spirits."

"Did he mention the Whitlock book at all?"

"No, I canna say he did." The geocacher's gaze turned towards the bar.

"Did he mention being worried about anything?"

Murray shook his head. "No."

"Where were you the night Lachlan was murdered?"

"I was home watching TV from eight until midnight when I went to bed."

"Can anyone verify that?"

Murray shrugged. "You'd have to ask my neighbours."

"Thank you, we will. And thank you for your time," McKenzie said, extending a hand across the table.

Murray's hand had a faint tremor.
The DI made a mental note.

4

SECRET SOCIETY

The mid-afternoon sun, streaming through the window, warmed the left side of McKenzie's face as he approached DCI Sinclair's cluttered desk. "Sir," he began, clearing his throat, "about the Lachlan Campbell case..."

Sinclair took his time to look up from his paperwork. Finally, he sat back in his chair, checking his watch. "Have you got any leads? It's been a few days."

Grant pulled a face, trying not to stare at the DCI's damp bald patch. "I thought we did, and now I'm not so sure. The more we delve into it this case, the more complicated it becomes. My concerns are about a rare book Lachlan was seeking..." He sighed. "I think someone killed him for it, but I am not yet convinced he actually had it in his possession."

"Go on," Sinclair leaned back in his chair, eyebrow raised.

"The book is supposed to be valuable not only because it is collectable as the author's lost work, but also because it contains encoded information about the whereabouts of the family fortune or an heirloom. People want it because of the information hidden inside."

"Why would someone kill Lachlan if he didn't have the book?"

"Maybe because they believed he did."

"And what makes you think he didn't?"

"Something one if his friends told me. He has never seen definitive proof the book exists. And we have been looking into this in depth, and cannot prove it did, either. At least, not yet."

Sinclair sighed. "Then I suggest you waste no more time on it. Look for other motives. Our foundation is evidence; hard facts. Perhaps this was a burglary gone wrong? Or maybe the killer had a disagreement with the victim?"

"Except Lachlan appeared to have no enemies. But he had many friends."

"I don't understand why someone would murder our victim for a book that doesn't exist. We are police officers, not conspiracy theorists."

"I understand what you are saying, sir." McKenzie shifted the weight between his feet. "But we cannot dismiss angles because they're unconventional. Regardless of whether Lachlan actually possessed the book, I think someone believed he did, murdered him for it."

The DCI's gaze drifted to the window, watching dust swirl in the sunlight. "Belief without evidence is dangerous, McKenzie. Be careful you are not chasing shadows. I need more than theories and conjecture. Where's the proof these encoded secrets exist? And how do you know the killer wasn't after any of the other dozens of rare books Lachlan had in his collection?"

The DI rubbed his forehead, knowing the DCI had a point. "I agree the evidence for motive is flimsy at this stage, but I'm convinced it points to something bigger. The insignia we found etched into Lachlan's floorboards wasn't random vandalism. I think it was deliberate."

"What makes you say that?"

McKenzie took a large print from the envelope under his arm and placed it on the desk. "This is what we found. The killer carved it. I think this is a badge. A sign of belonging."

"Like a secret society?" Sinclair raised an eyebrow.

"Yes, perhaps. I think it was a way for the killer to communicate with others."

"It could simply be the killer's signature, couldn't it? We may have a serial killer who is murdering victims uncon-nected to him."

"Except this insignia looks too specific."

Sinclair studied the symbols. "T K... The killer's initials? Or maybe they stand for 'The Killer'. He's probably messing with us."

The DI scratched his head. "I have to admit, I thought that too, at first. But it took time to carve that insignia, including the owl and the book. That isn't just a killer signing his initials... It has to mean more, in my opinion."

"So, what are you going to do next?"

"I have asked forensics to look into the symbolism. I'll see what they dig up." McKenzie's gaze remained steady.

"Fine," Sinclair murmured, setting down the photo. He fixed the DI with a cool look. "But beware of rabbit holes that lead nowhere. The clock is ticking."

"Understood, sir." McKenzie nodded, his jaw stiff. "I best get on."

The DCI pushed his hands into his trouser pockets. "Good. Keep me informed and don't stray into speculation without solid proof."

"Right." Grant turned on his heel.

"Good luck," Sinclair called after him. "A detective's greatest tool is his mind. Don't lose yours to gossip and conjecture."

McKENZIE STRODE BACK into the incident room, where his team huddled around the photographs and notes, spread across the whiteboard like a rapidly growing climbing plant.

"Quick chat," McKenzie called to them, a file tucked under his arm. "Can we go over what we have so far?" he locked eyes with each of them. "Lachlan's murder, the missing Whitlock book, and the victim's writings that seem to have disappeared into thin air... I believe these things are interlinked." He sighed. "Something bigger is going on here. I don't believe this was a robbery gone wrong. And at least one of Lachlan's close friends, geocacher Fergus Murray, believes Rosemary Whitlock never even wrote that book. He thinks the Whitlock Tome never existed." The DI ran a hand through his hair. "I'm telling you, this case gets stranger by the day."

"Maybe Murray was the one after the book?" Susan Robertson suggested, brow furrowed as she peered at the scattered evidence. "Where was he the night of Lachlan's murder?"

"Home in bed... Or so he says."

"Convenient... Any witnesses?"

"He's not sure whether his neighbours saw him. But we can ask them and check any CCTV in the street."

"I can look into that." Helen McAllister offered.

"Great, Helen. Thank you." The DI continued, "I want digital records pulled, bookstore owners interviewed, and anyone who's ever shown an interest in that book tracked down. We have to assume for the moment that the book exists. If it proves otherwise, then so be it. But the legend of the book is still an important thread, though it may not be the only one. Keep looking for other motives. According to his friends, everybody loved Lachlan. But someone murdered him. If we find out why, we find out who."

As the team dispersed, McKenzie made his way to the forensics lab where the symbol etched into the crime scene was being analysed. They had pulled in a symbology expert to study the enigmatic markings projected onto a screen, comparing them with photographs from the crime scene.

"What does it mean?" McKenzie asked, leaning against the doorframe.

Dr Martin Baird replied without turning round. "It's intricate and deliberate. I've been cross-referencing it with historical insignias, and I found this..." Baird handed him a copy of a black-and-white photograph he picked up from the desk. It appeared to be of an old bookshop. Above the entrance was an emblem that bore a striking resemblance to the one the killer had etched on the floorboards of Lachlan Campbell's attic.

"During the Second World War, a little-known history society in Edinburgh used the insignia." Baird tapped the photograph with his pencil. "They removed it in nineteen-forty-five, and the place reverted to a simple bookstore after the war ended. The sign and the history society fell into obscurity afterwards. But the insignia's presence at your crime scene has to be relevant."

"Do we know anything more about this history society?" McKenzie picked up the photograph, his eyes flicking between it and the projected crime scene photograph.

"Ah, that's where it gets murky," Dr Baird admitted. "Records are scarce, but it seems they were an enigmatic lot, and their interest in books and history could have been a front for something else."

"Really?"

"Don't you think it strange they left the premises after the war?"

"What about the symbols and letters T and K? Any ideas?" Grant ran a hand through his hair.

"It could relate to the group's name, which I haven't been able to find. But the Owl and Book likely refer to a secret knowledge they either had or sought. They wrote nothing down. Which is very odd. No meeting minutes, and no ledgers or books with anything in them."

"Were they Masons?"

"Perhaps some of them were, but I don't think that had anything to do with the society. And the Masons do not mention the group anywhere in their records."

"I see. Do you have any idea why they moved from the bookshop after the war?" Grant asked, scrutinising the image of the shopfront.

"Not really," he answered. "Perhaps some of their members were killed in the war, causing the society to disband," he answered.

"Could the book in the insignia represent the Whitlock Tome?" McKenzie asked, looking for a potential connection to Lachlan's death. "Lachlan was interested in a book written during the First World War. And now we have a potential connection with The Second World War." He straightened up, handing back the faded image. "Can you dig deeper into this society? Find out what they were up to? And whether someone might kill to keep whatever it was they did or had a secret? Maybe they had the Whitlock book at some point?"

"Aye, of course." Baird nodded. "I'll see what I can do."

McKenzie lingered, staring at the insignia for several seconds. Then, with a firm nod to the expert, he went to find DS Robertson.

As the car navigated Edinburgh's streets, the city's historic stone facades went unnoticed, both detectives deep in thought. The DI tapped the steering wheel, while Susan picked her lip, musing over what Baird had said.

"You know, maybe they were using the old book shop to hide criminal activity. Maybe they were buying and selling on the black market? The society could have been a front for it." The DS shrugged, gaze locked on the road in front.

"Perhaps," McKenzie acknowledged, his tone pensive. "But what has that to do with Lachlan Campbell and the Whitlock Tome?" He frowned. "What if the society didn't disband after all? What if they continued in a different location? Perhaps buying and selling rarities on the black market? It could explain why they might murder Lachlan for the Whitlock book?"

"If it was for money, maybe they were after the whereabouts of the fortune they thought Rosemary had encoded in her book. We know David and Rosemary were childless. But, after Rosemary's death, surviving relatives divided the known estate. Each family member had an equal share. I don't see how anything would be available for would-be fortune hunters to find. Unless there was an undisclosed pot somewhere."

"Did you notice how everyone mentions Lachlan's obsession, but no one admits to knowing anything about the notes he was writing?"

"Aye..." Susan pursed her lips. "Either his friends are

hiding something, or our victim kept his cards very close to his chest."

McKenzie's blue eyes narrowed. "Perhaps something in his writings got him killed?"

"Maybe he unravelled the secrets of Rosemary Whitlock." She nodded. "And it was information worth killing for, even after all these years."

McKenzie let out a deep breath as the car rounded a bend into creeping fog. "We keep digging, Sue. Lachlan's writings must be somewhere. So we keep looking."

The DS nodded. "I'll check the Edinburgh archives for information about that shop, too."

"Good." McKenzie turned the steering wheel as Leith Police Station came into view. "I need something to give Sinclair."

5

THE LOCAL HISTORIAN

McKenzie's gaze swept over Edinburgh's skyline, darkened by black thunderclouds. A cool wind, carrying the scent of rain-soaked cobbles, tugged at his coat as he and Dalgleish made their way to see a local historian.

"If anyone can shed light on the Whitlock lineage for us, it's Stella MacLeod." Graham said, as they approached the historian's shop on the Royal Mile.

The door groaned, and a bell chimed as they entered the glass-fronted former shop that was now a tiny museum. Inside, the space appeared cluttered but homely. Towering shelves stood lined with books and relics, and more books and maps lay in piles across a worn Persian rug. A middle-aged woman approached from a room at the back, pushing her glasses on top of her head. She straightened her skirt and blouse.

"Mrs MacLeod?" McKenzie walked towards her.

"Och, Stella will do," she replied, placing the book she'd been holding onto the desk and walking over. A slender woman with silvering hair in an elegant bun, her keen eyes appraised them with academic curiosity.

"We need your expertise," the DI began. "We wondered what you know about the Whitlock family, and Rosemary Whitlock's famous missing book." He held up his ID. "DI Grant McKenzie and DC Graham Dalgleish, Edinburgh MIT. We're investigating the murder of Lachlan Campbell."

"Ah, the Whitlocks..." Her eyes narrowed. "What is it you're wishing to know?" Then, almost as an afterthought, she added, "I was sorry to hear about Lachlan. What a shock it was..."

"Aye..." He nodded. "It was an unusual crime in these parts."

Stella shifted the weight between her feet.

"Can you tell us anything about Rosemary's book?" Dalgleish asked. "If it exists? And what it contains if it does? We understand Mrs Whitlock returned to Edinburgh to live after her husband died?"

A moment's silence followed as Stella considered the request, her fingers idly tracing the spine of a book on the desk. "Aye, that she did. I might have one or two things here that could help you," she said finally, turning towards a shelving unit containing multiple folders and documents tied together with string. "She lived close to here, actually, on the edge of Dean Village. Mrs Whitlock kept herself to herself mostly, according to papers of the period." She shrugged. "Writers can be a bit like that. It's a solitary profession, you ken."

"Aye, of course." McKenzie flicked a glance at Dalgleish.

"She was still very young when she died. Thirty-two... It's no age." Stella pulled out a file, blowing the dust off it before leafing through its contents. She stopped at a faded black-and-white photograph, now sepia with age, pulling it out with reverence, as though concerned about disturbing the folks captured within it. "Here they are, the Whitlocks... Rosemary and David, before he left for France." She handed them the photograph. "His family had a deep-rooted military tradition."

The DI gazed at the image. Rosemary, in a dark Edwardian dress, appeared shy and diminutive, hands clasped together, as she stood beside her tall, handsome husband clad in full uniform. He appeared confident, optimistic even, chin held high like so many of the young men who went off to war and never returned. Turning the photograph over, he read the simply penned annotation. 'David and Rosemary, on the outbreak of war, 1914.'

"You say David's family had a long history with the military?"

Stella nodded. "Aye, that's right... He came from a long line of fighting men. That family lost more than their fair share of blood over the years." She sighed. "David and his cousin Johnathan both perished in The Great War. It was a terrible blow to the family, one from which they never fully recovered. They were childless, you ken... David and Rosemary... She never remarried. They said she kept hoping, until the end of her young life, that he would come home. Missing in action, presumed dead, was the official verdict. So many men still lie in fields obliterated by explosions out there in France. They are finding and identifying remains to this day. Everyone knew he was dead, but his wife kept the flame burning, not even so much as looking at another man. They say she died of a broken heart, though her death certificate said pneumonia."

"Such a shame..." Dalgleish pressed his lips together. "And a waste."

She handed the DI more papers from the same folder,

aged but meticulously preserved and annotated. Among them were newspaper clippings, contemporary with the author. "These should provide you with further insight, Inspector."

McKenzie nodded, frowning in concentration as he scanned the documents. "Thank you, Mrs MacLeod. May we take these?"

"Aye, you can study them here as long as you need. There's a place over there." She pointed to a large table and chairs near the window. "But if you need to take them with you, I've a photocopier in the back room. I'll print off some copies for a fee." She pulled a face. "Sorry, but we need to pay for ourselves, you ken."

"Of course." He nodded. "If you give me an invoice, we'll get it paid."

She took the file into the back room, returning after five minutes with a freshly printed sheaf. "There you go."

"Thank you, Stella. We appreciate your help."

"Och, think nothing of it," she replied with a gracious nod. "I just hope it assists you."

With a last look around the room, a treasure trove of Edinburgh's past, McKenzie popped the papers under his arm. "We'll be in touch if we need anything further."

"Good luck in your search for the killer," Stella answered as they left.

Her gaze lingered on the doorway long after the two detectives had departed.

BACK AT LEITH POLICE STATION, McKenzie spread the documents over his desk, placing them in chronological order where he was able. The warm scent of freshly printed paper mingled with the aroma of coffee coming from a half-empty mug.

Dalgleish pored over the papers with him, grey-tinged hair catching the light as he tapped on a paragraph of an article. "See here," he said, running his finger along the words as he read, "Several Whitlock ancestors were high-ranking officers. The family was known for their bravery. It says here that, even when facing overwhelming odds, men willingly followed them into battle."

"They inspired true loyalty..." McKenzie's forehead furrowed. "Perhaps Lachlan stumbled onto something related to the family's military past? Something someone wanted to remain hidden?"

"I wish we knew what he was working on." Dalgleish scratched his head.

"Lachlan's friend Alistair MacGregor said it was something to do with meetings and David Whitlock. But he was really vague. He said he didn't read the pages properly when Lachlan asked him to."

"Or he doesn't want to tell us what he saw?"

"We'll speak to the cleaner again. If anyone caught sight of something more in his writings, it would be Sheila Fletcher." McKenzie straightened. "Maybe recovery from the shock will have improved her memory?"

Helen McAllister stepped into the room, blonde hair tied back, and glasses perched on her nose. She held up a manila folder. "I've been going through more of Lachlan's social media. He was a member of groups interested in geocaching and antique books. I've had a look through chats. As we know, he was part of a network of collectors and history buffs that were hunting the Whitlock Tome."

McKenzie leaned back in his chair, eyes fixed on the DC. "How extensive is this network?"

"As far-reaching as you get." McAllister flipped open the folder to reveal a series of printouts. "It's a worldwide phenomenon, and cross-referencing usernames and avatars takes time. It's a spider's web of interlinking connections, and not everyone goes under their own name. In fact, most people have nicknames and pseudonyms apart from the academics, who mostly use their proper names. I don't know if the nicknames are for privacy or fun, but I suspect it's a bit of both."

"What about Lachlan?"

"Lachlan used his first name, and a string of numbers based on his date of birth. It took a while to confirm it was him, but through a combination of IP address and his birthday, but we are now certain of the identification. Our techs are going through his computer and phone, which will provide us with more data."

"Is there anything to confirm Lachlan had the book?" Dalgleish asked. "Or anything to suggest its whereabouts?"

Helen nodded, taking a printout from the folder. "He put up several posts in the weeks before he died, first alluding to his knowledge of its whereabouts, and then to his excitement over seeing it for the first time." She handed the highlighted page to Grant. "Look for yourself."

He scanned the document, scratching his beard. "Okay, so either Lachlan really had come into possession of the Whitlock book, or he desperately wanted people to believe he had. I wouldn't say these posts were proof he had it, but it goes a long way towards supporting the cleaner's assertion that he did."

"I think we should talk to some of these collectors. They may know more." She closed the folder.

"Exactly my thinking." McKenzie stood, his back clicking as he stretched. "Helen, can you reach out to them?

Be subtle, at first. Whoever killed Lachlan will not open up about the book if they suspect we're police. We need to know if any of them made progress tracking down the tome, or whether any of them supplied it to Lachlan. If our victim had it, he had to have got it from somewhere. See if there is anything they can tell us."

"Understood." Helen nodded. "I'll approach it as a casual conversation amongst enthusiasts, and see how far it gets me."

"Aye, thanks. Keep me updated on progress."

"Will do." The DC picked up the folder and headed for the door.

"Careful, though," Dalgleish called after her. "Some collectors can be fanatical. Watch your back."

McAllister grinned at his concern. "I will," she said, stepping out into the corridor.

6

THE LOVE AFFAIR

"Sir, I have something!" Helen's eyes glowed as she placed her laptop on the DI's desk. "It concerns the rural hospital where David Whitlock was treated during World War I."

Displayed on the screen was an old photograph of a group of doctors and nurses standing proudly in front of a field hospital, along with several patients. The young man in front, seated in a wheelchair with a cast on his right arm, was unmistakable.

"That's David Whitlock..." McKenzie peered at the screen.

"Right..." Helen nodded. "I talked to a neighbour of Lachlan's, who chatted with him a week before the murder."

"Go on..."

She grimaced. "Trigger warning... This was tough to hear, given the suspicion his wife died pining for him..."

"Don't keep me in suspense." McKenzie grinned. "Spit it out."

"Apparently, Lachlan claimed to have found evidence of

an affair between David and the young nurse assigned to care for him in the hospital in Boulogne, after sniper fire injured him in Fromelles in nineteen-fifteen. I confirmed this with the casualty clearing station records. The hospital was a British field hospital, but French nurses who could speak English helped care for the injured. The woman's name was Yvette Fontaine." Helen pointed to the young nurse standing behind David, holding the handles of his wheelchair. "Lachlan alleged this lady is Yvette, and they fell for each other while she nursed him back to health. He was in the hospital for almost two months. Apparently Lachlan believed they started the affair in the hospital, but it continued after Whitlock's release. He went back to see her whenever he could until he went missing, presumed dead."

Grant frowned. "So, could this mean David survived the war, after all? Did he choose to disappear to be with this nurse?"

"I can't say, yet. All I know at this stage is that Lachlan was allegedly investigating this part of the story before he claimed to have located the Whitlock Tome. Oh, and one more thing, Lachlan mentioned a wee bairn."

"A child?"

"Aye, he said he was looking into a baby that was born to Yvette Fontaine early in the year that followed the taking of that photograph. That would have been in nineteen-sixteen."

"Jings..." The DI cocked his head, considering it for a moment. "So there could be an entire line of Whitlocks we know nothing about? And David Whitlock... What if he didn't die? What if he survived? What if he stayed with Yvette and the child?"

Helen pulled a face. "I've a lot of work to do, haven't I?"

"Aye…" He nodded. "We've certainly got our work cut out on this one."

Dalgleish pulled a face. "If Whitlock fathered a child with Fontaine, there could be untold numbers of descendants looking for that book."

McKenzie laughed. "The DCI won't be happy. Well done, Helen. I think we need to look deeper into this affair and its aftermath. Do we know if Rosemary Whitlock was aware of the affair?"

The DC shook her head. "It's on my to-do list to find out if she ever mentioned it, or if David ever wrote to her about it. I have found no mention of it so far, though."

"Fine, keep digging, Helen. That's some great work you've done there."

She nodded. "Thank you, sir. I'll start with local records, see if any of the existing relatives can shed light on this. If that trail runs cold, I'll reach out to our counterparts in France."

McKenzie parked his unmarked Vauxhall on a cobbled street in Edinburgh's Old Town. The ancient clock tower of the Balmoral Hotel struck ten, meaning it was three minutes to ten, as it had always run three minutes fast to ensure travellers would not miss their train. The air carried the damp chill of a Scottish spring morning, replete with mist, as the city's tourists began flocking to its sights.

He made his way toward the Canny Man's, pushing the door into its old-world charm. The smell of fresh scones and strong coffee teased his nostrils.

Sheila, Lachlan's former cleaner, sat in the far corner,

hands wrapped around a steaming cup. Her wide eyes watched him approach as she shifted in her seat.

"Mrs Fletcher," McKenzie nodded as he took a seat opposite. "Thank you for coming."

"Your call took me by surprise," she replied in a voice that rattled with phlegm. She cleared it, fingers tracing the rim of her mug. "I couldn't think why you'd be wanting to see me again..."

"Look, I know this will have been a hard time for you, Sheila, but can you tell me about Lachlan in the days before his death? I want you to relax and think back. You said you saw him writing notes. Were they in a book, like a diary? Or were they on loose pieces of paper?" he asked, head cocked.

She hesitated, then nodded. "Aye, I saw him scribbling away, always with that old fountain pen of his." She glanced down, twirling her wedding ring as she spoke. "He was writing something when I said goodbye that day, and he seemed particularly focussed, and talking to himself. He didn't look up when I walked into the room."

"And that was unusual?"

"Aye, he'd always look up and say hello or goodbye, and ask me how my day was. He was always friendly. But in those last days, he appeared completely engrossed."

"Did you see what he was writing? Did you read any of it?"

Her eyes shot to his face. "What do you take me for? I don't go prying into other people's business."

Grant held up his hands. "Och, I didn't mean you were being nosey. I just wondered if there was anything you could tell me about the notes and what he was scribbling down."

She thought about it for a moment. "There was a strange symbol thing..."

"Go on..."

"I saw it at the top of his journal page."

"Do you mean a drawing? Or was it headed paper?"

"Aye, he'd drawn it with his pen. It was like a circle... a queer sort of thing with letters and a bird in it."

McKenzie leaned in. She was describing the symbol carved next to Lachlan's body. Had she also noticed it carved beside her dead employer? "This symbol, did you recognise it from anywhere? Had you seen it before?"

"No, not before or since." She scratched her head. "I only saw it the once, on his papers." She cleared her throat again.

"And you are sure it was on the paperwork?"

"Aye."

"What else can you tell me about the notes? I believe you, when you say wouldn't deliberately read his journal, but did you spot anything at all? Any words that maybe stuck in your head?" The DI's voice remained calm, though his mind ticked over what she had said about the insignia.

"No, nothing." Sheila shook her head, eyes darting away. "Events are still a blur, I'm afraid. I can't believe he's gone... or that he was murdered. And I'm looking for more work to top up my income. He provided a sizeable chunk of my money. My head's been in a spin these last two weeks. I don't know if I'm coming or going."

McKenzie regarded her for a long moment, wondering if there was more beneath the surface she wasn't saying. She had been closer to Lachlan in his final twenty-four hours than anyone else save the killer. Could she have witnessed something vital, something she couldn't remember? "Alright, Sheila. If you recall anything else, you'll let me know?" His tone was courteous, but firm. "Have a think about it for me."

"Of course, Inspector," she promised, the quiver in her voice hinting at unease.

McKenzie stood, his mind churning. Perhaps Lachlan's killer had seen something in the bookkeeper's writings, something etched in ink that upset them. Was Sheila Fletcher an unwitting witness? Or did she know more than she was saying?

7

DAVID WHITLOCK'S BEST FRIEND

The clock hands inched towards three as DC Graham Dalgleish turned the pages of Stella MacLeod's meticulously kept archive on Rosemary Whitlock. The office was quiet, save for the occasional rustle of paper and the soft whirring of the fan on his computer.

His fingers traced the lines of text as he delved deep into the long-established pedigree of the Hugh-Wynstanleys, a family well-known to the Whitlocks. David Whitlock had been best friends with Quentin Hugh-Wynstanley since they were small boys. That friendship had continued until David's demise in France in nineteen-eighteen.

The Hugh-Wynstanleys had an extensive library, an archive that rivalled the collections of many a renowned institution. It was once said that when history whispered its secrets, the Hugh-Wynstanleys had them shelved and indexed before time could draw breath.

Dalgleish's keen grey eyes scoured an old newspaper article on the Whitlocks, where he learned of the enduring connection between the Hugh-Wynstanleys and Rosemary Whitlock. Despite the suspected death of her husband in The Great War, the article stated the family continued to correspond with the writer until her untimely death in nine-teen-twenty-nine.

He guessed their mutual love of David inspired the ongoing communication. However, according to the article, Rosemary had often stayed home when her husband dined with the Hugh-Wynstanleys. She wouldn't have been the only writer to prefer solitude, but Graham wondered whether Mrs Whitlock had not liked the family. However, the fact she corresponded with Quentin for several years after her husband's death suggested she had perhaps gotten over any reservations because of the friendship which had existed between David and Quentin.

The late Mrs Whitlock had already achieved literary acclaim long before David died in France. The Whitlock Tome was said to be a work of love; an homage to her dead husband. But had she encoded more than history in the epic work? Or was 'Whitlock' merely a celebration of her husband and his lineage? One thing he was sure of, the book was bound to have come up more than once in her correspondence with the Hugh-Wynstanleys. Perhaps the family's archive could shed light on the book, maybe even its whereabouts?

According to Stella Macleod's documents, the current heirs to the Hugh-Wynstanley estate were Horatio and William, who ran the country pile for their ageing father, Phillip. The estate included a working farm, housing for tenants, and much sought-after meat and dairy produce. It seemed the estate was a wealthy one, and the young men were in line to inherit the substantial legacy.

Dalgleish made a note to speak with the Hugh-Wynstanleys. If anyone could shed more light on Rosemary Whitlock and her book, it would likely be them.

"Bonjour, je m'appelle DC Helen McAllister, Leith Police Station, en Écosse," Helen spoke into the phone with formal courtesy, outlining her need to access French records.

"Merci beaucoup," she concluded, after the helpful officer on the other end confirmed they would give access to the documents she required once she emailed confirmation of her identity.

She peered at the growing dossier on Yvette Fontaine. Frowning in concentration, she opened the newly accessed files, delving into the digital archives with a single-minded resolve.

Fingers clacking on the keyboard, she chased multiple leads through the labyrinthine French archives, barely noticing as her colleagues left one by one, and evening drew in, accompanied by a mist outside her window.

She churned through entries of births, marriages, and deaths in Boulogne during and after the war years, pausing only to rub tired red eyes after pushing her glasses atop her head.

As she stifled a yawn, a birth register with a familiar name caught her eye. The child's mother was listed as 'Yvette Marguerite Fontaine', occupation — nurse, and the timeframe was right, but was this the one? Yvette had named the child David Jacques Pierre Fontaine. Helen was now sure she had found them. The nurse surely had to be David Whitlock's mistress, and her child — his son.

"Gotcha," Helen exhaled, sitting back, a thrill of excitement running through her. The fact Yvette had given her son David's forename, but her own surname, suggested she had not been willing to tell anyone who the father was. Her baby was almost certainly David Whitlock's child.

Helen gathered all the information she could on this Yvette Fontaine, carefully documenting her findings in a small file on the laptop. They included addresses and important dates. Yvette used her maiden name throughout. Was that because David died during the war, and she simply had not wanted to marry another? Had she lived with someone instead?

As she cross-referenced details with available public records and census data, the image of the woman who had captured David Whitlock's heart during the war became a little clearer. She imagined the nurse in her crisp uniform, a gentle hand on the captain's wounded brow as they shared stolen moments. Helen couldn't help thinking of her own search for a meaningful connection. What would she have done in Yvette's shoes?

"Let's see where you ended up, lass," she said, tapping into the local parish records.

Finally, she had an address near Boulogne, where Yvette had lived in the years following the war, in the historic town of Arras, one-hundred-and-twenty-seven kilometres from the former field hospital. Helen scribbled down the details, hands trembling at the significance of her find. The nurse's life had unfolded, revealing a child and potential heir of David Whitlock, born of their wartime affair. Could this be the thread leading to the motive for Lachlan Campbell's murder? Pieces were falling into place, although the true ending of David Whitlock's story was still elusive.

Leaving the office, the DC was almost too tired to drive,

but she smiled to herself, satisfied she had achieved a significant leap forward.

THE FOLLOWING MORNING, McKenzie found her yawning and pouring herself a coffee. "Any luck yesterday?" he asked, grabbing a mug to pour one for himself when she had finished.

"Aye, potentially," Helen replied, plopping a couple of sugars into her drink. "I got a fair amount of information, but it'll take time to check and cross-reference it all."

"Can you give me a summary?" He cocked his head.

"I've been digging into the French connection, as you know, the affair between David Whitlock and Yvette Fontaine. And I believe I have the identity of the child he may have fathered." She outlined the information she had gleaned from French records, stopping only to sip hot coffee now and again.

Grant listened, fascinated. "Wow, very well done, Helen. That's a lot to take in, but it means we have concrete information to follow up. Do you think you can see it through to the present day? Find out if there are current descendants we should talk to?"

"Aye..." She nodded. "I'll carry on with it today. It takes a wee while, but I hope to have something for you by this afternoon."

He pursed his lips. "The thing is, I don't really see how the French connection would tie in with a mysterious Scottish history society here in Edinburgh, or the insignia carved into Lachlan's floorboards."

"Maybe the murderer left that as a red herring?

Whoever this killer is, they'll have done their research right enough."

He nodded. "You're right, they almost certainly will have. Good work, again." McKenzie grinned. "I'd better watch myself... Sinclair might give you my job."

"Oh, go on with you." McAllister laughed. "I've got work to do."

8

THE UNWITTING HEIR

McKenzie leaned back, chair creaking under his weight as he scanned the report handed to him by Graham. The mid-afternoon sun filtered through the blinds, casting stripes of light and shadow across the DI's paper-strewn desk.

"I found quite a bit on the Hugh-Wynstanleys," Dalgleish began, folding his arms. "They were corresponding with Rosemary Whitlock long after her husband's presumed death. According to Stella's notes, there were upwards of twenty letters from the years leading up to Rosemary's own passing."

McKenzie raised a brow, interest piqued. "And Quentin was the one who was friends with David Whitlock?" he asked, eyes scanning the report.

"Aye... Thick as thieves, they were," Dalgleish perched on the edge of McKenzie's desk. "Quentin's great grandsons, Horatio and William, run the estate these days. It's a grand old place in Yorkshire, with a couple of hundred acres of land and a mansion with more history than most museums."

"Really?" McKenzie tapped his pen on the desk. "I wonder if they could shed some light on the book, and where to find it?"

"I think it'd be worth talking to them." Dalgleish nodded, his grey-flecked hair catching the light. "The elder brother looks after their father Phillip, the great-grandson of David's friend Quentin."

"And if they have such an extensive library, they are likely a mine of information."

"Exactly..." Dalgleish agreed.

HELEN APPROACHED THEM, looking pleased with herself. "Got a lead from our French pals," she said. "A descendant of David Whitlock and Yvette Fontaine. Goes by the name of Pierre Fontaine."

"Fontaine?" McKenzie raised a brow. "The family continued to use Yvette's name?"

She nodded. "Yes. She named her son David Fontaine. Pierre is from that male line. I also found out he's a frequent visitor to the UK. Comes over several times a year, apparently."

"Really? Where? Scotland?"

"London mostly..." She glanced at her notes. "But his business tendrils stretch far and wide, and he travels to other parts of the UK."

"We should talk to him." McKenzie rose from his seat, hands on hips. "Let's look into Pierre Fontaine's business, and what he does while he's here. Perhaps he's been looking for Rosemary's book, especially if he knows his origins, and has heard of the Whitlock Tome."

"I'll be chasing that today," Helen nodded. "Leave it with me."

McKenzie paced to the window, gazing at the buildings across the street. "Right, we've got two different threads to follow up. Let's get something concrete for Sinclair, before he hauls me in again for another dressing down." He grinned, looking over his shoulder at Dalgleish and McAllister. "My life is on the line."

A TELEPHONE BROKE the silence in the main office. Dalgleish lifted his eyes from the file he was reading and grabbed the receiver. "MIT, Dalgleish speaking."

Grant, who had been staring out the window and thinking, turned to face him. He watched the DC's mouth fall open, and the colour drain from his face as he listened to the voice on the other end.

"No way..." Dalgleish's voice cracked, his knuckles gleamed white where he gripped the receiver. He shot a glance at McKenzie and shook his head. "We'll be there right away."

As Graham hung up the phone, everyone stared at him.

McKenzie walked over. "Spit it out, man," he urged, brow furrowed with concern. "What the hell happened?"

"It's Fergus Murray," Dalgleish said, throat tight. "He's been killed in a hit-and-run. They found him on the road to the Lothians. It sounds suspicious, to say the least."

McKenzie took a moment to register it, fists clenching by his sides. Fergus had been one of Lachlan's best friends. Had someone deliberately snuffed him out? If so, why? "Damn it," he muttered. "Maybe the killer knew Fergus was talking to us?"

"Aye, perhaps someone was afraid of what he knew?" Graham rubbed his forehead.

"I'll drive." The DI grabbed his jacket. "We need to see this for ourselves."

"I'll come with you." Dalgleish stood.

Helen McAllister looked up from her research, face etched with concern. "Will you two be okay to cover it?"

"Aye." McKenzie nodded. "We've got this. You carry on looking into the French connection, and set up an interview with Pierre Fontaine for as soon as possible. If he is in the UK, I want to see him."

She nodded. "Will do. Be careful out there."

9

COLLISION ON A LONELY ROAD

N orth of Edinburgh, under a sullen sky, the countryside was a patchwork of rolling hills and windswept moors, dotted with ancient stone walls and cottages. Drizzle hazed the rugged landscape and, though lush with heather and gorse, the Lothian hills appeared to mourn the tragic events they alone had witnessed.

McKenzie pressed his lips into a tight line as he drove himself and Dalgleish along the winding lanes. Fergus's collision had not the luxury of CCTV like that afforded to Edinburgh's city streets. Unless another vehicle with a dashcam was passing, there would be no recording of the impact.

A chill breeze flapped their coats as they approached the grim scene on a road bordered by dense woodland. Fergus Murray's lifeless form lay broken, bloodied, and twisted on the cold tarmac. His bicycle, a crumpled mess, lay several feet away. The road was eerily silent, save for the occasional chatter of traffic officers and the distant call of a curlew. The traffic cops had already cordoned off the road with blue and white tape that fluttered in the wind.

"This was no accident," Dalgleish muttered under his breath, eyeing the scene.

"McKenzie..." An officer waved to them. He was standing next to forensic personnel, who huddled over the scene, photographing and measuring, their white suits crackling as they moved. The officer pointed to a set of dark lines on the tarmac. "Tyre marks here, and over there. I'd say there was a deliberate swerving towards the victim. It looks to me like someone intended hitting him."

The DI crouched, observing the dark rubber scars, forehead furrowed. They told the story of the driver's trajectory and the vehicle's violent manoeuvres. "Speed?" he asked, scouring the road.

"Fast enough to kill," a forensic officer replied, face partially obscured by a mask. "Impact suggests the vehicle was doing approximately fifty to sixty miles per hour. They didn't brake until after the impact, and that seems to have been only to come back and see the damage."

"Looks deliberate," McKenzie affirmed, sighing as he ran a hand through his hair. He traced the path of the tyre marks with his eyes, noting their abrupt, intentional swerves. The marks were about seven feet apart, showing a wide, erratic turn before the deadly impact.

The forensic officer nodded. "We measured fifteen feet for the initial swerve and a further twenty for the follow-through. Blood spatter analysis suggests the point of impact was there." She pointed. "The victim was knocked off his bike and thrown several feet through the air, landing where he is now. There are fragments from the car's light casings and metallic silver paint which we can analyse. But the perp left the scene, heading north."

Dalgleish made notes. "We'll get a message to all units in the area, find out if they saw a vehicle being driven erratically, and ask for any CCTV from the few houses around here. You never know, one of them may have captured something. We'll have all eyes looking out for the damaged vehicle. I hope we get to it before they patch it up, eh?"

"Tyre marks suggest he may have had another go." The SOCO officer stood to her full height.

Grant frowned. "They hit the victim again, to make sure."

She nodded. "That's what I'm seeing on the road. It's possible they were manoeuvring to get themselves out of there but, maybe, they tried hitting the victim again."

"Christ!" Dalgleish ran a hand through his hair. "That's some evil bastard, eh? I hate to think the victim might have still been conscious throughout all that."

The SOCO shook her head. "I doubt it... It was a helluva first impact. If they came around and did it again, I'd say it was probably to make sure."

THE TWO DETECTIVES drove most of the way back in silence, lost in their own thoughts.

The DI finally thought out loud. "Fergus didn't deserve to die like that." He shook his head. "He seemed a decent bloke. But I will say he seemed nervous when I talked to him in the Canny Man's. I wonder if he knew this might happen?"

"What, that someone would try to get him?"

"Aye... He told me he thought the Whitlock Tome didn't exist. But what if he was just trying to put us off looking for it? Maybe he knew more about the book's whereabouts than he was letting on? Perhaps he was terrified he would be next, after Lachlan, or worried about where our investigation was heading."

"So are we assuming that Lachlan's killer was also the driver of the car that hit Fergus? It's still possible this was a freak accident?" Dalgleish suggested.

"Aye, we can't rule out an accident at this stage, but what sort of accident leads to the driver hitting the victim again? Some accident that would be." McKenzie pulled a face.

"I ken, but the person may have panicked. Maybe he wanted to make sure the victim couldn't give us the registration number. I'm not saying the driver wasn't a killer, but he may not be the same one who murdered Lachlan."

"Aye, but what are the chances, eh? More likely, this was our killer. But, if so, why Fergus?"

GRANT AND HELEN sat across from Pierre Fontaine in the interview room.

McKenzie could see from the information sheet prepared by McAllister that Fontaine was a forty-two-year-old Antiques dealer who travelled frequently between France and the UK.

The DI took in the dark hair flecked with grey; sharp eyes; and a thin nose and chin. The tanned man opposite appeared shrewd and mentally agile as he surveyed them both. He wore an expensive-looking white cotton shirt with an Italian-style collar, and pale brown chinos. He appeared relaxed and comfortable, like he had all the time in the world.

"You can understand my surprise when Helen told me

you were in Edinburgh." The DI's eyes narrowed. "We wanted to speak with you, and there you were."

Fontaine blinked both eyes, his face a mask. "I often visit Edinburgh. I have been here many times over the years." He shrugged. "Why not? I'm an international dealer, and travel to many capital cities. I have done this for decades. Edinburgh is a city with a rich history. How do you say... It's right up my street." Fontaine smoothed the table with his fingers. "I've found and sold some excellent pieces here." He spoke with a French accent, but in perfect English, like a native had taught him.

"Had you heard of Lachlan Campbell?"

Pierre's eyes narrowed. "Who?"

"Lachlan Campbell. He spent his life collecting rare books." McKenzie watched for movement in the dealer's face and body, but detected none. Fontaine was giving nothing away. "He died recently."

Still not a flicker.

"Actually, someone murdered him."

Blank look.

"A thin metal garrotte to the throat."

"Look, I'm sorry... What has that got to do with me?" Pierre shrugged. "You are getting to something, I can see. Say it, please."

"Quite a coincidence, your visit aligning with Mr Campbell's murder." Perhaps this last was unfair, but the DI was probing, looking for any sign of recognition.

"Coincidences are merely patterns created by the universe," Fontaine countered, slow-blinking both eyes once.

"Did you know him? Lachlan?"

"No."

"He was interested in antiques too, you know..."

"Was he?"

"Books, mostly."

"Ah, I rarely chase down old books. I'm more a paintings and sculptures man."

"We understand he spent most of his life hunting one book in particular."

"Really?"

"Yes... You might have heard of it... the Whitlock Tome?"

Fontaine swallowed; his fingers began tapping an erratic rhythm on the table.

"Does that title ring any bells with you?"

"I might have heard of it on my travels, I can't be sure."

"People from around the world have been searching for it for nigh-on a hundred years."

"Wow..." Pierre leaned back in his seat. "So, why are you talking to me?"

"Where were you on the evening of Tuesday, the ninth of April?" McAllister asked?

"Er, let me see... Tuesday..." His eyes fell to his lap as he considered his answer for several seconds. Finally, he looked up. "I was at an art gala, here in Edinburgh, as it happens. At the Scottish National Gallery. It was one of the main reasons I was here in the city, actually." Fontaine shifted in his seat.

"Can anyone verify that?"

"Yes, probably at least twenty people. You can check with the gallery. They will have the names of those who were there. And I can give you a list of the guests I spoke to."

"Thank you. We will take names from you before you leave." McAllister nodded. "What time did you leave the gallery?"

"Er, around midnight? I guess. Could have been eleven thirty..."

Grant and Helen exchanged glances. It fit the timeframe. The DI shifted focus. "Tell us about your family."

"What would you like to know?"

"Where you grew up? You speak perfect English."

"I grew up in Boulogne. My family moved there from Arras when I was young. I still spend most of my time in Normandy. It's easy to go between France and the UK on a ferry. I fly sometimes, but I am not a fan. I prefer water. If there is an accident, you can at least swim for a while but, up there? Well... You know."

"And your excellent English?"

He shrugged. "Most of my family are dual language speakers. It's not so unusual in that part of France."

"What do you know of your ancestors? Your great-great-grandfather, for instance?"

Fontaine frowned. "I don't understand. Why are you asking me about my great-great-grandfather? Do you know much about yours?"

McKenzie grinned. "Touché."

"Then what?"

"Have you ever heard of Rosemary Whitlock?"

"Er, she was a writer, wasn't she? If I remember rightly?"

"She was. She wrote the book Lachlan was seeking."

"I see..."

According to reports, the book focused on the Whitlock family line, including her husband David Whitlock, who went missing in action in nineteen-eighteen while fighting in France.

"Oh..." Pierre looked as though the penny had dropped. "That is why you are asking me about my family? Do you think they hid this David Whitlock?"

"He had an affair with a young nurse."

"I don't follow..."

"Her name was Yvette Fontaine."

"Wow." He ran both hands through his hair. "Of course. The love affair. I heard something about it when I was young. My grandmother told me the story. She said it was Yvette and a young English soldier called David. She had a son."

"Right."

"Who was my great-grandfather. I have always had an affinity with the UK."

"What did your grandmother tell you about Yvette and David?" McKenzie's gaze was steady and open.

"Just that there was an affaire de coeur, a love affair during the war that produced a child. And that my great-grandfather resulted from that union." He shrugged.

"Did they know what happened to David?"

"If they did, they didn't tell me. But, clearly you think this David Whitlock was my ancestor."

"You said you might have heard of the Whitlock Tome?" McAllister prodded.

"It rings a bell, but not because my grandmother told me about it. She didn't. If it is internationally sought after, then that is how I will have heard of it."

"It went missing when Rosemary died in the late nine-teen-twenties."

"I wouldn't know anything about that. If it exists, it is probably in some collector's vault somewhere. A private collection."

"What do you mean, if it exists?" McKenzie's ears pricked up. Did Fontaine know there was a question mark over whether the book was ever written?

"I didn't mean to imply anything by that. You said people have been searching for it for nearly a century. That makes me wonder whether the book is real, that is all."

His answer did not entirely satisfy the DI, but for now, he let it ride. "How long do you intend staying in Edinburgh, Mr Fontaine?"

"I am here for another few days before I return to France."

"And when will you be here again?"

"That will depend on whether there is something in a catalogue or exhibit I want to see. So, I can't say."

"Fine." McKenzie nodded. "We'll take that guest list from you before you leave. Thank you for coming in today to speak with us."

"No problem, Inspector."

"WHAT DO YOU THINK?" Grant asked Helen when they returned to the office.

"It's hard to tell. He's difficult to read. I think he knows more about that book, though. I'd put money on it. But he didn't react to the news of Lachlan Campbell's murder, did he?"

"No..." The DI shook his head. "Either he really does know nothing about it, or he has supreme control over himself."

DR FIONA CAMPBELL pushed stray hair back from her face, before masking up and putting on latex gloves in the Morgue of St Andrew's Hospital, in Edinburgh.

Hair tied back in a bun, she stood over the stainless steel examination table where Fergus Murray's broken and lifeless body lay, his pale skin bruised and mottled.

"Are you ready, Grant?" She asked, adjusting her glasses.

McKenzie cleared his throat, notepad in hand. "Aye, I'm good."

She adjusted the overhead microphone, ensuring it would capture all she had to say as she worked. "Right, I'll get started... Our victim is a Caucasian male, twenty-eight years old. The cause of death seems to be trauma from a vehicular collision. Beginning with the external examination."

The pathologist reverently moved the young man's head, revealing significant damage. "I can see on the right side of the head a large bruise and lacerations to the right temple, where his head impacted the ground. The skin also has gravel embedded in it, which is consistent with the tarmac road where the victim was discovered."

Grant took a step closer, wanting to see for himself. "Is there a way to tell if the collision was deliberate?" he asked.

"We'll get to that," she answered, without looking up. "But don't get your hopes up. Let's look at the rest of the body first."

Fiona continued her examination. "There are abrasions, contusions, and torn skin along the arms and legs, consistent with sliding across a rough surface. He certainly hit the road at speed." She looked up at the DI. "You would think, if this was an accident, the car would brake, and slow down prior to hitting him. But this was a high-speed impact." She moved to the chest and abdomen. "Multiple rib fractures, here, here, and here. The pattern supports the idea this was a high-impact collision. Given the placement, it looks like the vehicle struck him from the front, left-side. Likely the victim had swerved, trying to avoid the impact."

McKenzie nodded. "But could any of that show intent?"

Fiona paused, looking at the DI. "It might. The angle

and impact force imply the vehicle didn't just clip him; it hit him with considerable speed, and while the victim was trying to avoid it. Of course, we can't rule out the driver was simply speeding, and became distracted, not seeing the victim approaching on his bike."

"I see..."

"Let's check the back." Dr Campbell carefully turned the body. She would normally have help at this stage, but her assistant was having a routine pregnancy scan at Edinburgh's Western General.

McKenzie would have helped in a heartbeat if suitably attired. Instead, he cleared his throat as he watched Fiona cope without fuss.

The pathologist continued. "There is deep bruising across the lower back and crush damage with some patterning."

"What would have caused that?" Grant cocked his head, taking further notes.

"Well, we rarely see this in an accidental hit-and-run, but we have seen it on murder victims. I think he was struck again, post-collision. This looks like a tyre mark to me." She took photographs and measurements as Grant peered at the markings. "And here," she pointed to the bruising on the backs of his arms. "These could be defensive wounds. He may have been conscious and trying to protect himself."

She turned the body back to its former position before opening the chest cavity and abdomen to examine him for internal injuries. "The broken ribs punctured the lungs, and there was significant internal bleeding... The heart is undamaged, but the liver is lacerated, which is another sign of significant blunt force trauma."

"So, collision at speed, and likely at least one more attempt to hit him whilst he was prone on the ground." The

DI pulled a face. "The bastard," he said, referring to an unknown perpetrator. "It makes it worse, eh? The thought the victim was possibly aware after the initial impact. Anything else about the injuries you think are significant?"

Fiona paused, wiping at her forehead with the back of her wrist. "The patterning here is key. The injuries suggest this was likely more than an accident; there's a brutality to this; signs of deliberate action. The angle at which the car struck him on the second occasion would suggest the driver turned the vehicle's wheels, as he hit again him again."

Grant pressed his lips together. "Someone wanted him dead."

"Aye, it would seem so. We'll need the toxicology results to find out whether the victim was under the influence, but the physical evidence so far suggests he didn't stand a chance either way."

McKenzie nodded, sighing. "I think this is the same killer as the one who murdered Lachlan Campbell. We need him off the streets. This callous bastard won't stop till we catch him."

"Well, you and your fine team are the best people for the job." She left the table, taking off her gloves. "I'll finish up here and get a report over to you tomorrow."

"Thank you, Fiona, you are a star."

"Och, I'm no star, but I know you'll want to shift on this. I don't want to be the slow cog in the machine."

He laughed, a guttural sound from his belly. "You a slow cog? Never."

10

HIDDEN ARCHIVE

T he winter sun cast long shadows across the rolling Yorkshire moors as McKenzie and Dalgleish approached the wrought-iron gates of the Hugh-Wynstanley estate. The ancestral home lay inside, its quiet grandeur a stark contrast to the grit and throng of Edinburgh streets.

"They canna be short of a bob or two," Dalgleish muttered, eyes scanning the imposing pile as McKenzie drew to a halt on the sweeping gravel drive.

Horatio Hugh-Wynstanley, twenty-eight, greeted them at the door. His youthful face seemed at odds with his confident air, height, and deep voice. He led them through vast corridors adorned with portraits of imperious ancestors, several in military uniform. The air smelled of beeswax and the musty smell of antiques.

"We'll go through to the library, if that's okay. Our father has fallen asleep in the drawing room." Horatio's confident steps clacked on polished floors as he led them down a long corridor. "It's his age," he added, grimacing.

Grant and Graham exchanged glances.

"William is waiting for us there," he said, referring to his twenty-six-year-old brother.

Heavy oak doors framed the entrance to the Winston Hall library. Inside, the scent of old furnishings mingled with that of polish and antique books greeted them. The room was vast. Ceilings soared twenty feet above, with elaborately moulded light fittings and cornicing on the ceiling. The walls were a pale yellow, and the room was lit by an enormous pair of Georgian windows, either side of which were long cream velvet curtains held back by thick, gold-colour ties.

"We have one of the most comprehensive libraries in Yorkshire." Horatio grinned. "We have our forebears to thank for that." He showed the two detectives to plump leather chairs at a central table at least five or six metres long, where his brother William sat, notepad and pen at the ready.

Row upon row of towering bookshelves stretched floor to ceiling, each hand-crafted from dark, lustrous wood. A rolling ladder affixed to a rail reached the highest shelves, allowing access to the rarest volumes. Many of the books were bound in faded leather, others in cloth, their spines embossed with gilded titles.

Nearby, an ornately carved fireplace provided warmth, its mantel adorned with pre-historic pieces such as ammonite and clay pipes.

The only wall not lined with books displayed yet more portraits of ancestors who watched those seated at the table.

"We have several first editions here." The younger Hugh-Wynstanley extended his hand. "I'm William. Pleased to meet you."

Fair-haired, in contrast to his brother, the younger Hugh-Wynstanley was also smaller in stature, though not by much. Large biceps stretched the material of his shirt, and McKenzie suspected both brothers availed themselves of a home gym somewhere within their vast country seat.

"I believe DS Robertson spoke to you two days ago, to explain the reason for our visit?" Grant pulled out his notebook.

"She said something about us having information in our library that could help with an investigation." Horatio perched on his chair sideways, the back of it under his right armpit, as he regarded the detectives with an open stare.

"That's right." Grant cleared his throat. "We are investigating a murder that took place in Edinburgh two weeks ago. The victim was a collector of rare and antique books."

The brothers exchanged glances.

"What has that to do with us?" William asked.

The DI continued. "The victim, Lachlan Campbell, had spent a long time searching for a book connected to your great-great-grandfather's best friend."

Horatio frowned. "Our great-great-grandfather's friend?" He shrugged. "You've lost me already."

"David Whitlock was best friends with Quentin, your relation."

"The Whitlock boys looked up at a portrait on the wall of a man looking imperious in a military uniform, with blonde hair and a moustache."

"Is that him?" Dalgleish asked.

"That is Quentin Hugh-Wynstanley." Horatio nodded.

Grant continued. "David Whitlock was believed to have been killed in action in France in nineteen-eighteen. His wife wrote a book about him before she, too, died young. The book went missing after her death, and our murder victim spent his life looking for it."

"I see..." Horatio nodded. "So, how do we and our

library fit in? We don't have the book, if that is what you are thinking?"

McKenzie held up a hand. "That's not why we are here, though it is interesting that you stated that without first checking your shelves. Had you heard of the book before?"

"What book are we talking about?"

"If you don't know which book, how do you know you haven't got it?"

"We don't have any of Rosemary Whitlock's books here in our library."

"Really?" McKenzie rubbed his chin. "A famous local author, who knew your family well; whose husband was your ancestor's best friend, and you do not have even one copy of her books?"

Horatio shrugged. "Well, I guess our family didn't purchase any of them. You are talking about events long before our time."

The brothers exchanged another glance.

"Your family corresponded with Rosemary after the death of her husband. Your great-great-grandfather kept in touch with her. Did you know that?"

"We might have heard something about it before. I couldn't give you the details, though," Horatio answered. "I have to confess to never giving it much thought."

"Me neither," William added.

"Our victim told others he had come into possession of Rosemary's homage to her dead husband. The book she titled, 'Whitlock'. And we wondered if Lachlan Campbell was murdered because he found the only copy of it, or someone believed he had it. The book has been much sought after internationally and it allegedly contains something of great value, connected to David's story, within it."

"I still don't see how we fit in." Horatio shifted in his chair.

"We were wondering if your family has any of the letters exchanged between Rosemary Whitlock and Quentin Hugh-Wynstanley, particularly during the war years and the decade following. Or any that passed between Quentin and David Whitlock. If we know more about the book and its contents, we might learn more about the motive of the killer or killers of the collector, Lachlan Campbell."

"I see." Horatio scratched his head. "Well, it isn't our library you'll be wanting. It's our muniment room... Our family archive. That's a different animal all together. We can show you that, if you like?"

"That would be helpful, thank you." McKenzie nodded.

"It's right here." Horatio stood. "We wouldn't normally do this, but... since you are police officers, this is our muniment room." He crossed to the bookshelf opposite and pulled on a gilded volume bound in faded red leather.

That part of the bookcase, extending from the floor to half-way up the wall, opened outward to reveal a far smaller room containing basic shelving, boxes, dusty volumes on tables, and row upon row of annotated lever-arch files.

Horatio motioned for them to join him.

"Wow." Dalgleish stood. "I wasn't expecting that."

William laughed. "We almost wore this door out as kids. We didn't care a stuff about the dusty old books but, as soon as we discovered this room, we were addicted."

Horatio nodded. "It was great for hide and seek."

"Aye, I'll bet it was." McKenzie walked inside the archive, scanning the shelves as he went. "I take it the letters are in here?"

"They are." The older brother nodded. "Which years are we talking?"

"Nineteen-fourteen to nineteen-thirty should cover it," The DI answered.

"Fine... They should be in these files here." He pointed them to a row of folders with the relevant dates. "Well, if there is nothing further we can help you with, and we can trust you, we will leave you too it. If you pull that cord when you have finished..." He pointed to a bell in the corner. "One of us will come back to see you out. Oh, and... We would ask that you remove nothing from the room without our express permission."

"May we photograph documents if we find something useful?" Grant asked.

The brothers looked at each other.

William shrugged. "Fill your boots. The files are labelled with the relevant years. I'm afraid you'll have to wade through other family correspondence too. We'll trust you not to read anything that isn't pertinent to your investigation."

"One more thing, before you go..." The DI took his mobile phone from his pocket, flicking the screen until he found what he wanted. "Have either of you boys seen this before? And can you tell us what it is?" He held the phone towards them, the screen displaying the round insignia carved in the floorboards near Lachlan Campbell's body.

William and Horatio took turns peering at the screen; looking at each other before shaking their heads. The older brother frowned at McKenzie. "Sorry, I do not know what that is. I've never seen it before. What is it?"

"That's what I was asking you."

"Sorry, we have no idea." Horatio shrugged.

"Thank you, anyway." Grant put his phone away. "We'll be getting on then," he said, grabbing a file from the shelf as the brothers left, and taking a seat at the round table underneath a small window.

Dalgleish grabbed another file before joining him. "Right. We'll get started, shall we?"

"Aye, we've got fourteen or fifteen years to get through," the DI answered, already flicking through letters from nineteen-fourteen.

"I COULD DO WITH A COFFEE." Dalgleish put down a file to rest his eyes for a moment. "I have found nothing in this one so far."

"Me neither. I'm surprised, I thought there would have been a few letters written early in the war, at least." McKenzie looked at the DS. "But, from what I have seen, I suspect Quentin Hugh-Wynstanley did not go to the front straightaway, like David did."

"No?"

"No... It looks like he was involved in business meetings in Edinburgh, Liverpool, and London, on behalf of the family. I know he went to the front, because of the information Stella MacLeod gave us, but it must have been later. There are a few letters to and from his family while he was at the front, but none from nineteen-fourteen."

"I thought we weren't supposed to be reading anything that wasn't related to David or Rosemary Whitlock."

"I didna read it." Grant grinned. "I scanned it."

Graham laughed. "That wouldn't get you off in court."

McKenzie continued. "Quentin's younger brother Daniel was an officer with David in Fromelles. There's a letter here between Quentin and Daniel. Looks like Daniel was there early on, and Quentin joined them at the front later. Maybe he relied on his brother to relay his messages to Whitlock in the early days?"

"Have you read it?"

"No, but I'll take a photo, and we can examine it when we get back." The DI checked his watch. "Keep going. We've got a lot to get through."

Twenty minutes later, and Dalgleish found the first correspondence between Quentin and David Whitlock. "Got something... a letter from Quentin direct to David, and a reply from David, two weeks later."

"Get photos," McKenzie ordered. "We'll have to get a shift on, or we'll never get through this lot and get to Rose-mary's letters as well."

"Got it." Dalgleish nodded, taking out his mobile to snap the documents.

McKENZIE AND DALGLEISH scrutinised high-resolution images of the letters discovered in the hidden muniment room of Winston Hall. Ties loose, and hair messy from copious hand-combing, they placed pieces of conversation together like a jigsaw puzzle. Dalgleish sipped cold coffee, having forgotten it was there.

"Graham, look at this phrasing," McKenzie murmured, tapping his finger on one sentence in a letter so well preserved it could have been penned the day before. "The winds blow cold on my heart, but still I trust my husband will make it home safe, Quentin. I would rather not hear that he has suffered a bullet to the back. You wouldn't appre-ciate the consequences, were that to happen."

He frowned. "What did Rosemary mean by that? Was she concerned about potential treachery in the trenches?"

Dalgleish read the sentence over. "If I remember rightly, from my modest knowledge of The Great War, some officers were afraid that when ordering their men over the top, they might themselves receive a bullet so the lads could deny being given the order. Could that be what she is referring to? What rank was David Whitlock?"

"He was a captain in the British Expeditionary Force."

"Then that would make sense, wouldn't it? Perhaps she was afraid his own men would shoot him, so he couldn't order them over the top. Wasn't Fromelles a subsidiary to the Battle of the Somme? They underestimated the strength of the German defence, or so they taught me in school."

"Why would she threaten Quentin?" McKenzie asked, tone serious as he turned to Dalgleish. "She tells him he wouldn't like the consequences."

"Well, he would lose his best friend, right?"

"I think there's more to it... Rosemary Whitlock wasn't penning sweet nothings to David's best friend, that's for certain. I sense tension between them... veiled, but present. If so, what was the reason?"

"Perhaps there was a previous romantic involvement? Or an affair?" Dalgleish ran a hand through his hair. "I agree. There is some sort of current running under the layers of etiquette, but it's natural for a wife to be anxious. She was pressuring Quentin to help keep her husband safe. He would have seen him regularly, as they were both captains. Maybe she thought he could keep an eye on him, or keep him out of harm's way?"

"David was a good soldier and, from what I have read in these letters, a committed one. I doubt he would have accepted any favours, even if they were offered. He seemed an honourable man." McKenzie sighed. "But we still have no confirmation of the Whitlock Tome's existence, or any suggestion of who might have taken it if it did."

"Quentin had motive, perhaps?" Dalgleish suggested, pulling at his lip. "A falling out with Rosemary may have soured him enough to want the book, especially if he didn't come off well in it?"

"Exactly what I was thinking..." The DI pushed his hands into his trouser pockets. "If Quentin had a part to play in whatever happened to that book, these letters could be the key to understanding why."

"Perhaps it had something to do with how David died?" Graham shrugged. "Though we know there was never confirmation of his death."

"And we also know there was an affair that produced a child. And that complicates things." Grant sighed. "Let's keep digging. Lachlan Campbell believed the Whitlock Tome existed. And I believe the killer did, too. Real or imaginary, someone wanted that book so badly he or she was prepared to kill. And, given a person or persons knocked Fergus Murray off his bike, they may have killed again. "

"Traffic has Fergus's case, for now, don't they?"

"They do, but I want us to liaise closely with them. Fergus's death was no accident."

11

MURDER IN THE PARK

Grant's phone cut through his concentration like a blade, making him jump. He answered it with a nod at Dalgleish. "McKenzie."

"Sir, are you able to take a call? I have a Stella MacLeod on the line."

"Go ahead." He looked at Graham, brow furrowed. "It's the historian-"

"Are you there?" The female voice sounded nervous and unsure. "I'm wondering if you've time to see me?" She paused, breathing laboured. "It's about the insignia you've been looking into. That circular sign you showed me. I think I've found something."

"Really? What?" The DI could hear distant traffic on the other end. Stella was outside somewhere.

"I've a lot to tell you, and I think you'll want to see for yourself."

"Very well..." McKenzie drummed his fingers on the desk. "Shall I come to your office?"

"No." She delivered the word like a bullet. "Can you come to Inverleith Park? Do you know the Sundial Garden?

I'll meet you there." She paused, sucking in a breath as though fearful of something.

"Are you okay, Mrs MacLeod?"

"Half an hour." She ended the call.

"Right..." The DI put down his phone, turning to Dalgleish, brow furrowed. "Stella thinks she's onto something," he said, getting to his feet. "She wants to meet in half an hour. Says she has something for us. She seemed unsettled."

"What about the letters?"

"We can continue going through them when we get back."

"Where are we going?" Graham rose to his feet.

"Inverleith Park... The Sundial Garden. We've got less than thirty minutes." McKenzie's tone mirrored the storm clouds looming outside, dark and heavy. "She seemed scared..."

"Right, we'd better go." Dalgleish grabbed his jacket.

THEIR RAPID FOOTSTEPS synchronised on the stone steps to the street, the ominous sky amplifying their sense of urgency.

"Stella didn't come across as someone who would spook easily." Graham opened the passenger door of their unmarked vehicle.

McKenzie slid behind the wheel, hands gripping it as he contemplated Mrs MacLeod's meagre words and the way she delivered them. "Aye, I think whatever she found has her rattled. She didn't want us going to her office."

"You think she worried about someone seeing us there again?"

"Maybe."

The engine roared to life as they pulled away from the car park and into the mid-morning traffic on Queen Charlotte Street. Skirting the bustling waterfront at The Shore, they took a sharp right onto Bernard Street, the historic Leith Theatre momentarily looming in the rearview mirror, before they plunged into the chaos and frustration of Leith Walk's congestion.

Once free, they roared past the grandiose Fettes College, its Gothic towers silhouetted against the stormy sky, before veering left onto Inverleith Place. Finally, Inverleith Park came into view.

Grant checked his watch. The journey had taken around fifteen minutes. "She said she'd be on a bench overlooking the water ten minutes from now."

"Might as well get there and wait then, eh?" Dalgleish suggested.

"Aye, let's go." McKenzie nodded.

NEITHER MAN SPOKE until they began walking over the grass towards the secluded Sundial Garden.

"Feels too quiet," Dalgleish murmured, eyes darting around as they approached the rendezvous point.

"She's keeping a low profile," McKenzie replied, moving with purpose along the gravel path through the trees

As the Kinloch Anderson sundial came into view, with its four stone faces and bronze gnomons, surrounded by low-lying iron railings, so did the surrounding benches. There, on one seat, partially obscured by the reaching branches of a conifer, sat a solitary figure with her back to them.

"Stella?" McKenzie called, cocking his head as his feet crunched gravel.

No response.

"Stella?" He ran towards her, gut clenched, a chill creeping up his spine.

She had slumped forward, head bowed as if in prayer. A thin wire, visible against her pale skin, had embedded in her neck amidst bloodied scratches where she had desperately tried to pull the weapon from her neck. The garrotte had cut into her flesh, leaving angry bruises and mottled reddening. The whole told of the awful and brutal end to Stella MacLeod's life.

"Christ Almighty," Dalgleish swore, feeling for a pulse; instinctively reaching for his radio.

"Wait," McKenzie held out a hand, keen eyes scanning the surroundings. "She can't have been dead long." He knew better than to disturb the scene before forensics arrived, but every fibre of his being screamed that the killer must be close. Maybe even watching them. "God damn it," he exhaled sharply, the realisation they had arrived too late lying like lead in his stomach. Someone had silenced Stella MacLeod to stop her talking. His gut instinct that she was afraid had been correct. But they still hadn't reached her in time. "Can you hear that?" he asked Graham.

"Hear what?" The DC held his breath.

"The traffic... That's what I could hear in the background when she called me. I think she was already with her killer. Go ahead, call it in. Let's get the area secure. No one comes near until they've processed the scene."

While uniform and forensics cordoned off the Sundial Garden and park beyond, McKenzie's gaze lingered on Stella's unmoving form. She had been a historian holding keys to the past. It must be the reason someone murdered her.

That, and whatever she had found out about the enigmatic insignia found near Lachlan's body. They needed more on the secret history society that had melted away like heated butter after the Second World War; information someone wanted to prevent them from having.

MCKENZIE CLENCHED HIS FISTS, jaw muscles jumping as he fought the anger welling inside. He was sure the killer was taunting them — forcing Stella McLeod to call, all the while knowing she would not be alive to talk when the police arrived.

"Whoever did this knew exactly what they were doing," McKenzie muttered, voice thick with emotion. "I think the murderer knew what we were looking for."

"A killer willing to risk exposure in this way is going to make a mistake." Dalgleish reassured, though experiencing similar concerns. "We just need to stay alert. He's going to slip up."

When the forensics team arrived, McKenzie watched the park transform into a meticulous search grid and tented crime scene. He watched them take careful samples and dust everywhere for fingerprints, photographing everything in precise detail.

"Look at where she's positioned." He turned to Dalgleish, pointing. "This was all designed for maximum impact. We were supposed to believe she was simply relaxing on the bench, right until the last minute. The killer set this up to shock us... Like a threat."

"Which leaves us not knowing for sure whether she knew anything."

The DI nodded. "We'll go through her home and office.

If she had information, she may have left evidence behind for us to find."

Dalgleish nodded, eyes on the victim. "And the garrotte... It looks to be the same type used on Lachlan. Bespoke, I think? Not your average piece of string. We should check local shops and online purchases again, although the searches turned up nothing after Campbell's death."

"I suspect someone made it in their workshop. The wire could have been in a garage for years. But, yes, we'll check for recent purchases. No stone unturned."

McKenzie's mind whirled. Had the killer followed Stella out here to the park? Or had he lured her from her office before forcing her to make the call to the police? The answer to that question would have told him whether Stella really had important information about the insignia. If someone simply lured her and forced her to make that call, then it's possible that she didn't have the information she claimed to have.

The wind had picked up. Any moment now, the heavens would open. Grant crouched beside the park bench, his gaze sweeping the grass stretching out behind it. If he wasn't there already, the killer likely approached from behind, while Stella waited for the police. Beside the scratch marks on her neck, there were no signs of a struggle. Perhaps he had accompanied her on the walk; making small talk, all the while knowing he would end her life in one stealthy act, as silent and deadly as the one that took out Lachlan Campbell. "Look at the ground here," he murmured. "Not a blade out of place. Our murderer slipped in and out like a ghost."

Dalgleish nodded. "There are prints in the mud, but looks like many feet have been through here, and probably a teenager party last night. I doubt they'll get anything useful, but you never know."

Heart heavy, McKenzie made a mental note to contact Stella's family, even though the words would stick in his throat, both because of their grief, and the responsibility he felt at involving the historian in his search for answers. He had spoken with Fergus and Stella, both of whom were now dead. That did not sit at all comfortably.

"Let's get back to it, Graham," he said, sad eyes taking one last look. "We have work to do."

As they prepared to leave, the DI's phone vibrated in his pocket. It was a text from his wife Jane, a simple heart emoji, a reminder of the life that kept him grounded. He smiled, pocketing the phone. Thank God for her.

12

ONE OF OUR OWN

Finishing later than most of her colleagues, Susan Robertson stepped out of Leith Police Station, buttoning her coat against the rain she expected at any moment as thunder ripped through the sky.

The street was quiet save for the storm, and the distant hum of city traffic as she headed for her car along a close next to the station. As the sky darkened, streetlights sprang to life, casting long shadows over the pavement. The staccato rhythm of her heels echoed off the walls.

The DS yawned, rummaging for car keys in her bag. It was almost nine o'clock. She hadn't intended working late, but their current case was a minefield, with information oozing from every pore. Getting data wasn't a problem, but sorting fact from fiction was. Many of the answers appeared rooted in a long-forgotten history, which only made things harder.

A flicker of movement caught her eye. Susan turned. It was only the flutter of litter along the pavement — an innocuous crisp packet and paper bag. She exhaled. Perhaps the storm had made her jumpy. The sight of her car did nothing to quell the unease that chilled the back of her neck. A coiled tension settled in her stomach as she approached the vehicle.

"Get a grip, Robertson," she murmured, senses heightened. Yet the quiet isolation set off a prickling sensation down her spine; the feeling of unseen eyes on her. That was the curse of her profession, the knowledge that darkness sometimes harboured more than mere shadows. She picked up pace, the car now fully in view; keys clenched in her fist, ready to unlock the tiny sanctuary as soon as she reached it.

In the distance, obscured by the darkness clinging to a recess between buildings, a figure dressed in black watched the DS's every move. Waiting. Breathing muted by a mask whose fabric blended seamlessly with the void. The watcher's meticulous nature rivalled Susan's own. Patience was essential for what he needed to do. As the storm's lightning flickered, the figure made his move.

He kept to the edges, a phantom flitting outside her peripheral vision. Steps measured. Calculated to match the DS's pace. A safe distance. A buffer zone allowing observation without risk of discovery. He was a master of this dance, moving with ease.

DS Robertson pressed her key fob. An answering click signalled the unlocking of the door. In the otherwise silent close, she swung it open with more force than intended, driven by intuition to escape the dark spaces. She paused. A fraction of a second. Senses straining to find the source of her anxiety. A presence. A footstep behind, close enough to make her catch her breath.

Before she could react, a hand clamped over her mouth with crushing force. The scent of leather gloves invading her nose. Her training kicked in, and she tried twisting away, elbow aiming for what she hoped would be her attacker's stomach, but the assailant fended off her move with chilling efficiency.

The struggle was silent save for the scuffing of shoes on cobblestone and the strained breathing of predator and prey. Panic surged within her, wild and hot as she fought against the stifling hands. Her usually ordered thoughts raced in chaos. Greg's face flashed in her mind, his warnings about safety haunting her. But the masked man smothered her screams under his oppressive gloved hands, focussed only on the outcome. As Susan fought against being smothered, she felt her consciousness fading.

With one last effort she fought back, bucking and writhing to survive, the cobblestones cold and unforgiving beneath scrabbling feet now devoid of shoes. "Let go of me!" she grunted, the words muffled against his vice-like grip. Her hands clawed at the masked face, seeking purchase on anything that would give her leverage. It was like grappling with mist; his head pulled back, leaving only the Leith night air.

She had trained for this, had gone over scenarios repeatedly with her partner, Greg. But nothing prepared her for the disorienting terror of being the target and not the protector.

His strength did not flag, his movements deliberate and calculating. A knee drove into the small of her back, sending a shockwave of pain through her body. The ground rushed to meet her, her head colliding with cobblestones. That was the last thing she felt, the passionless kiss of stone against her temple. Then nothing. The figure stood over her for a moment before disappearing down the close.

IN THE QUIET of his office at Leith Station, McKenzie waded through the case file, a cup of coffee going cold on his desk. Everyone else had left for home. Soon, he would go too. The phone jolted him from his thoughts.

"McKenzie," he said, standing to look through the window at the waning storm.

It was the front desk. "Just received a call from Sergeant Boyle. DS Robertson's been attacked. She was found unconscious just off Bernard Street. She's alive, but injured. There's more... the attacker left a note in the hood of her jacket."

"What?" McKenzie's gut clenched in dread as he listened, heart sinking like a stone in the Firth of Forth. His mind conjured images of Susan, bruised and bloodied. "Where is she?"

"In the Western General," came the answer, referring to Edinburgh's largest hospital.

"Make sure we have officers posted outside the ward. I'm on my way," McKenzie commanded, voice calm despite the turmoil inside. "And I'll want to see that note as soon as possible."

He ended the call, standing motionless, the gravity of Sue's predicament belting him like a gut punch. The killer they were pursuing was no ordinary adversary; but a calculated, audacious psychopath, willing to confront the police head-on. And now, that killer had delivered an ultimatum.

DI McKenzie grabbed his coat, grinding his teeth. He would not let this attack go unanswered, and he would not abandon the investigation. They would find this perpetrator and quell the storm hanging over Edinburgh. "Stay strong, Susan," he murmured, stepping out into the drizzle. "I'm on my way."

13

DARK DAYS

The attacker had left a crumpled piece of paper inside the hood of Susan Robertson's jacket — "Stop your search or face the consequences."

The perpetrator had laser printed the words on paper bought from a large online batch. Thousands of packs of that paper had been delivered, hundreds in Edinburgh alone, making it virtually impossible to trace the person who printed it.

Below the threat sat an insignia. The same one carved in the floorboards next to Lachlan Campbell's body.

DS Susan Robertson was lucky to be alive.

DI McKenzie stopped a nurse on the way out of the ward. "Can I see her?" he asked.

She shook her head. "She isn't awake right now. The doctors sedated her and will carry out more tests tonight. But, so far, all seems positive. If you come back tomorrow, she may be sitting up. It looks like she's going to be okay. But she'll need time."

"Thank you." McKenzie turned towards the uniformed

officer by the door. "Stay vigilant," he ordered. "And call me if there's a problem."

GRANT SAT at the kitchen island, hands clasped around a mug of tea, with a far-away gaze and soulful eyes.

Jane watched him from across the table, heart reaching out in silent support. She didn't speak, not wanting to disturb her husband's thoughts, preferring to wait for him to sort through them and be ready to talk. She gently stroked the back of his hand.

"Jane," he said finally. "This case is a mess." He set down the mug, running both hands through his hair and sighing. "People are dying, and Susan is lying in the hospital. Some bastard is running around killing and harming with impunity, and I am failing in my duty of care. He's running rings round us, love. It's as though he anticipates our every move, taking out witnesses before we even know their significance."

His gaze fell onto the cooling liquid inside his mug, as though seeking answers from within it. "This isn't our typical investigation. He's made it personal."

Jane nodded, her fingers brushing over his. "Grant, love, you've faced down some of the worst this city has to offer, and you've come out stronger each time," she said, her words delivered in the soft Scottish lilt that always helped calm him. "You've a knack for finding truth. Few can match it."

He looked up, the piercing blue of his eyes meeting hers. "It feels different this time, love. They've harmed one of our own; this is a direct threat to stop us pushing forward with the case. They are letting us know they can strike at will.

And two of our witnesses are dead." He shook his head, looking tired and pale. "We dropped the ball."

"They've picked on the wrong team," she replied, rubbing his arm. "You won't let that darkness spread. I know you. You're the man who doesn't back down, remember? You and your team must be more careful now... Stay vigilant. But you are strong, and you have a good team. You will crack this case and get your killer. If anyone can, you can. Just promise me you will keep safe. Think of the children and I. We couldn't bear to lose you."

He nodded, giving his wife a gentle smile. Her faith in him had always been unwavering. She was his anchor in times like this, helping him navigate the minefield of his own doubt. "Thank you, Jane," he whispered, taking a large swig of tea before turning his full gaze on her. "We'll take this killer down."

"Of course you will. And I'll be right here to support you, every step of the way. You do whatever you need to. Only promise me to be safe."

14

A SHOCKING CONNECTION

McKenzie's brow furrowed as he pushed aside the police tape and stepped over the threshold of Stella MacLeod's office. The chaos within had him gasping.

Papers fluttered in the breeze from a shattered window. Pens, ink, and other stationary lay scattered and spilled across the room. Books, their spines damaged, lay strewn across the desk and floor. Someone had pulled out and tossed the drawers. They had gone to town looking for something. The DI rubbed the back of his neck.

Graham Dalgleish let out a low whistle. "Christ, what a mess," he muttered, eyes skimming the carnage.

They donned latex gloves, wondering where to start amidst the dog's dinner that had been the historian's ordered room.

"Somebody spent a while in here." McKenzie fished his mobile phone out of his coat pocket, calling the station to report the break-in.

Graham nodded, the light from the window picking out the grey at his temples. "Whoever did this was looking for something specific. She had something they wanted, don't you think?"

"Maybe..." They began searching through the rubble, careful not to disturb the evidence more than they had to, and photographing items in situ when they needed to move them. McKenzie's eyes focused on a filing cabinet with yanked-open drawers, its contents lying in jumbled heaps on the floor. "Perhaps it was Stella's written records they were after?"

"They came round the back to avoid being seen... Smashed the window." Dalgleish's gaze wandered the room, following the route he believed the killer took. He pointed towards the jagged glass left in the window frame. "But it's too obvious, eh? The mess they left... It's like they wanted us to know they had been here. If this was the killer, they could have searched without destroying everything."

The DI nodded. "Looks personal, doesn't it? Whoever it was, they were angry with Stella." His attention was now on the papers that carpeted the floor. He knelt, picking up a sheet to read it. The writing was a scrawl, and hard to make out. "These look like notes she'd been keeping daily. Gather as many of these pages as you can. There may be something in them to tell us why this happened."

"Aye, okay."

"Were they looking for the Whitlock book, I wonder?"

Graham pulled a face. "It's hard to know what was taken if you don't know what was here to begin with. Perhaps she had the book all along."

"Let's go through everything," McKenzie instructed. "If she had it, she would most likely have hidden it well. There's no saying the killer found it. Perhaps they made this mess in frustration because they didn't find it."

"I wish she had told you what she had found regarding the insignia. We might know what we're looking for."

"Aye, and she wanted to meet in the open; not here in her office."

"Do you think she was worried someone was watching her?"

"I think it's likely. It would have been easier to meet here, but she rode on buses to the park, changing several times on route. That tells me she was trying to put someone off the scent, unless the killer forced her to do all of that. But, like you, I wish she had found a way to let me know what was going on."

They continued sifting through the remnants of Stella's work, bagging anything they thought might help them in their search for her killer. McKenzie picked up a photograph that had fallen amongst papers from a lever-arch file. The edges were dog-eared, the faded faces captured in monochrome. Four men, smartly dressed, probably from the nineteen-thirties or forties. He gazed at it a moment, wondering about the people; what their stories were. He checked the back, but there was no annotation. He placed the image back where he found it.

"Anything?" Dalgleish asked, yawning despite himself.

"Nothing that stands out." McKenzie shook his head. "Time's moving on. Let's get over to Stella's home. Forensics will be there, and they will be here soon." He checked his watch. "If she has the Whitlock Tome, it may be in her house. Let's hope the killer didn't get there before us."

McKenzie's gloved hand lingered on the brass knob of Stella MacLeod's front door, the cool metal polished to a shine. With a nod from Dalgleish, he pushed it open. They crossed the threshold, moving police tape aside with practiced care.

A plastic-suited crime scene officer approached. "Nothing disturbed, and no sign of a break-in."

"Have you finished here?" The DI asked, standing aside to allow the officer and his colleague to pass.

"Aye, we're off to the break-in at the victim's office."

McKenzie nodded. "We've just come from there. It's a mess."

"Och, we'll look forward to that." The man pulled a face.

"Let me know if you find anything." Grant turned his attention back to Stella's home. Unlike her office, there was no chaos to greet them, only a clean, well-kept home. And, based on the lines in the carpet pile, Stella had vacuumed the home before she left on the day she was killed.

"It feels like she just left," Dalgleish said, eyeing antique furniture in the hallway. "She certainly liked old pieces."

"This is odd..." McKenzie frowned, stepping into Stella's tidy but comfortable living room, with its soft furnishings and large bay window.

"What is?"

"An intruder, likely the killer, upends all of Stella's office looking for something. But they don't bother searching her home? Really?"

Graham scratched his head. "What are you thinking?"

"They were certain that whatever they were looking for had to be connected to her work as a historian and record-keeper. It looks like they didn't think it would be at her home. They expected it to be in her office."

"So it's unlikely to be the Whitlock Tome..."

"Right... Because she would be just as likely to have that

hidden in her house as anywhere. Perhaps they were after information, and not the book?"

"You have a point." Dalgleish nodded.

"Keep your eyes peeled, anyway," Grant continued, scanning the room as he negotiated the thick Persian rug.

The living room gave an insight into Stella's lifelong interests. History seemed woven into each item of decor. The walls were adorned with framed letters and prints, each representing a different time period. Reproductions of ancient maps sat alongside nineteenth- and twentieth-century ones. In a mahogany bookcase were rows of old books, most without sleeves. Dalgleish read the titles, double-checking the Whitlock Tome wasn't amongst them.

McKenzie's gaze lingered on a set of original blueprints for Edinburgh's old town. Stella's penciled annotations lay along the margins.

"Look at these…" Graham stood near another bookshelf, groaning under the weight of leather-bound volumes. His gloved finger traced the spine of a particularly worn book, its title embossed in faded gold: "Clan Histories and the Jacobite Uprising."

"Stella lived and breathed this stuff." McKenzie sighed, his respect for Mrs MacLeod growing by the minute. "Edinburgh lost a mine of information with this lady's passing."

"Aye, right enough," Dalgleish nodded. "And she had no children to pass her knowledge on to. Still, I expect almost everything is on the internet these days, eh?"

"I expect so." The DI's thoughts turned briefly to his childhood, remembering how certain teachers brought their subjects to life. He would always rather listen to their vivid retellings than read a cold textbook or encyclopaedia. As his eyes wondered over more of Stella's collections, he couldn't help feeling like an intruder. She had been a private person;

not one for going out except for work. And, after her husband passed away from multiple sclerosis four years prior, she had not attempted to connect romantically with anyone else. Perhaps she considered her collections and hobbies enough, in contrast with Lachlan Campbell, who relished getting out and about, and had many friends coming and going.

"Come on, Stella," McKenzie muttered. "What was it the killer needed? What did you have that he wanted so desperately?"

Dalgleish had his back to him, examining a collection of letters bundled together with faded ribbon. He opened several, scanning their contents. Some appeared to be the love letters of Stella and her husband while they were courting. Others could have been those of family members, going back at least a hundred years. Several were written during the wars. "Did you know Stella's name was Wallace before she married?" he asked Grant.

"Was it? That was Rosemary's maiden name, too. I wonder if she was any relation?"

"She kept letters from the family going back decades," Graham murmured, holding up a grainy photograph of a war-torn street, possibly in France, extracted from one letter. "There's one here penned in Normandy."

"Really?" The DI crossed the room to see.

"Aye, she seems to have kept a lot from the wars, first and second. There's someone who could have been her grandfather, perhaps? A Finlay Wallace, writing to his cousin in Normandy during the Second World War."

McKenzie examined the envelope. "This was sent from Edinburgh."

"Aye, looks like it."

"So this Finlay Wallace wasn't fighting?"

"No... He says here, his munitions factory could barely keep up with demand. He was obviously busy at home."

"There's so much here. But does any of it explain what happened to her?" McKenzie sighed. "See if there is anything relevant to Rosemary Whitlock or her book. Stella knew something and I think the killer silenced her because she was going to pass that on to us, something to do with that history society, no doubt. Keep looking."

"Aye, will do."

There were not enough hours in the day to go through every volume or letter on the bookshelves.

They read more only if they believed a title or date was of interest. However, nothing stood out as being potentially related.

"I'm going to the back room." McKenzie ran a hand through his hair.

Dalgleish nodded. "I'm about done here, too. I'll join you." The pair entered a room which Stella had clearly used as a study. Another bookshelf lined with old volumes occupied most of one wall, and an oak desk occupied a space underneath the window, looking out over a small garden. Notepads, pens, and recent bills lay where Stella had left them. The DI switched on the Victorian-style brass desk lamp and began flicking through the notebooks, looking for anything that might explain what information the historian had wanted to pass on, and the reason she was murdered.

Dalgleish investigated the bookshelf, gloved fingers moving down the spines as he worked his way along. "Here's something, I think?" He stepped back. In his grasp was a journal, the pages filled with a mix of long- and shorthand. "Stella wrote in this recently," he said, flipping to the most recent pages.

"Let me see," McKenzie accepted the notebook from his

DC. He couldn't read the shorthand, but knew Helen McAllister would be able to, her having been a personal assistant before joining the force. "Let's get this back to the station." The DI bagged the diary in plastic. "I'll ask Helen to have a look."

"Good idea," Dalgleish agreed, casting a last glance around the room. "I'll ask them to leave the police tape across the door for at least a week, in case we need to come back."

GRANT TURNED THE PAGE, eyes narrowing as he read Helen's translation of the shorthand scrawl Stella had used to encode her thoughts.

Opposite, Dalgleish flicked through letters and photographs, brow furrowed in concentration until he finally looked up. "I think we need a coffee... Is anything jumping out at you?" He queried, placing the letter he'd been reading down on the desk.

"Bits and pieces..." McKenzie scratched his head. "She mentioned a meeting, and had written 'urgent info for McK.'" And that's me, obviously. He shrugged, but there is nothing here to suggest what that was... Unless I'm missing something. She wanted to tell me something about the insignia urgently, but reasons known only to her didn't want to tell me on the phone or pop into the station.

"She must have thought it safer to meet in the park." Dalgleish exhaled, the air flapping his lips. "She knew she was in danger."

"Or she was already with her killer, like we thought." McKenzie flipped through the pages. "But I canna find anything in these entries to say what the information was."

"She was afraid to write it down, in case someone found it." The DC shrugged.

"But why? She lived alone. Who was going to read it? Who, or what, was she protecting it from?"

"Likely whoever killed her. She may have worried they would enter her home, like they did her office."

"I wish she'd left us some breadcrumbs." McKenzie continued sifting through the pages, working his way back through several weeks, sighing every once in a while at finding nothing to help them.

Graham plopped a mug down on his desk. "This is strong. It'll put hairs on your chest and keep you awake."

"Thanks." The DI sat back, rubbing his eyes and resting them for a minute while he gingerly sipped the hot liquid.

Dalgleish donned a fresh pair of latex gloves and picked up another of Stella's letters from the bundle he had taken from her house. His fingers caught an old photograph tucked between the sheets of paper. He carefully extracted it, holding it up to the light from his LED lamp. The photo had yellowed with age, its edges curling and frayed. "Wow... look at this," he said, passing it to McKenzie. "What do you see?"

The black and white, grainy image showed four men gathered in what looked like a study, next to shelving and books. Their dark suits made the figures pop on the faded paper, as though they could step out of the photograph and into the present.

The DI's gaze lingered on the faces, each one smiling, their camaraderie clear. Whatever meeting they were at was evidently going well. Their postures were relaxed, yet there was a clear formality to their dress, giving the impression something important had transpired in their coming together. Their stances told of camaraderie and shared purpose. The first man, with a confident smile, had his arm draped casually over the shoulder of the chap beside him. There was a twinkle in his eye, the kind that hinted at secrets only they were privy to. Next to him, a stern-looking individual with a hawkish nose stared at the camera, lips in a taut line. The other two were younger, but important-looking — shoulders squared to the camera, an unspoken challenge in the way they held their chins.

"I've seen these people before." McKenzie frowned "I can't think where..." He looked at Graham. "Who are they?"

Dalgleish nodded towards the photograph. "Keep looking... What else do you see?"

There was a moment's silence as The DI studied the image.

"Bloody hell!" Grant sat upright in his chair, holding the photograph up to the light from the window. "Is that what I think it is?"

"Looks like it to me." Graham nodded.

On the wall behind the suited men, partially hidden from view by the shoulders of the middle two, the insignia of the mysterious history society.

McKenzie cross-checked it with a photograph on his computer of the sign scrawled next to Lachlan Campbell's body. "This is it," he said, "but who are the men in this photo?" He frowned, thinking. "I think I know where I saw these men before... It was a photo in Stella's office. It fell out of a large file. We need to know where this was taken, who these men were, and whether they were associated with that insignia on the wall."

Dalgleish passed him a sheet from within the letter.

The DI examined Stella's neat, cursive handwriting. "Old Edinburgh History Society," he read aloud. "Founded 1914." Then, among the names, "Finlay Wallace, Treasurer. Dieter

Schmidt, guest of honour, 1942." He frowned. "But why are only two of the men named? Who were the others? Stella told us this enigmatic history society was based in a bookshop in Edinburgh's Old Town. I'll contact the library, find records for shops in that part of Edinburgh during the war years. We'll find out who those men were, and what the significance of this meeting was. Dieter Schmidt was a prominent member of the Nazi party, wasn't he? What business had he in Edinburgh in nineteen-forty-two? And with this society? And why had Stella been so intent on documenting it?"

"Well, her grandfather's involvement would be one reason," he said, pointing to Stella's own words. "But why was he involved with someone like Schmidt?" Dalgleish's voice was a low rumble. "What in God's name was going on?"

"Let's get this photo tagged and bagged," McKenzie agreed, renewed urgency in his voice. "All roads seem to lead back to that society."

15

SINISTER LINKS

Susan was sitting up in her hospital bed in the Western General when the nurses finally allowed Grant in to see her.

"Hey, I hope he came off worse." He grinned. "I've known some excuses for not coming in to work, but this trumps them all."

She laughed, then winced, hand going to her side. "Och, go on with you. I wasn't expecting this when I worked late the other night."

Grant's expression sobered. "We have CCTV of the attack but, unfortunately, we don't see the attacker's face. We know his build and have a good approximation of his height... You did well to fight him off as long as you did."

She rubbed the back of her neck. "He came out of nowhere."

"How are you feeling?" Grant perched on the end of her bed.

"I've got a massive bump on my head. That's why I'm still here. They scanned it to make sure I'd no got a brain bleed.

But I'm hoping to be let out later today. I'll be back at work tomorrow."

"Oh no, you won't." The DI put his hands on his hips. "You need to recover. I admire your dedication, Susan, but we can cope without you for the rest of the week."

"There's nothing broken. They've vetted me thoroughly. I've just a few wee bruises and sprains."

"Did you recognise his voice?"

She shook her head. "No. But I'm not sure he was Scottish. There was a bit of an accent, but he only growled a few words. He could have been disguising his voice, eh?"

"What sort of accent?" Grant frowned, mind ticking over.

"Ach, I dunna ken... Just no Scottish. English, maybe?"

"Hmmm..." The DI made a mental note. "Did uniform take your statement? I noticed they still have an officer posted in the corridor. That's good. I don't want the attacker having another go."

"Aye, I gave a statement. I'd better go through it, though, because I was on powerful painkillers, so I wasn't the full ticket. I've still got a bit of a headache when the meds wear off."

"You definitely need rest, young lady." Grant grinned. "Seriously, Sue, it's good to see you looking so much better than you did when I came in the other night."

"You came here? I Didn't see you."

"No... You were out of it."

"Och, of course. Well, I'll see what the doc says later."

"Have you got someone picking you up, or do you need a lift? Call me. I'll come straight here."

"Thanks, Grant, but Greg's taken the day off. Proper worried, he was. He'll be in shortly. He'll get me home all right. I'll be champing at the bit next week to come back."

"Good." The DI nodded. "Well, I better get on."

"Aye, watch out for big burly men with strange accents."

The DI laughed. "I will."

"WHAT YOU GOT FOR ME?" Grant asked Graham and Helen when he got back to MIT.

Dalgleish looked up from his work. "Dieter Schmidt, in civvies, hobnobbing with a secret society, and not a swastika in sight," he answered. "If he was here on clandestine business, there'll be more to it. I'm finding out all I can about secret Nazi trips to the UK."

"Aye, great, but have we got an ID for the two unknowns in the photo?"

"Not yet, but that might come the further I get into this. I've been looking up far-right activity in the Britain during the Second World War. We know there were friendships going on. Even the British Royal Family had at least one secret talk with the Nazi's, but I think that was maybe more an attempt to broker a peace deal. I mean, I get it. Look at us, now. We all travel abroad. We have friends from other countries. If a war broke out, could we suddenly decide our friends were now enemies? I mean, it couldnae have been easy."

"Sure..." The DI nodded. "But you said you were looking into far-right groups in Scotland?"

"In Britain, aye. Look at this." Dalgleish read an annotation from Stella's journal. "'Friend of Oswald Moseley?' That can't be coincidental. Put that together with this photo, and the one you found in Stella's office, and we could be looking at Nazi sympathisers... Maybe this history society was a cover, put together to further the aims of the British far-right, whose leader was Oswald Moseley, as we know."

"Far-right ties," McKenzie nodded. "Stella was onto something... something that got her killed. Dig into everything we can find on this group, and Stella's grandfather Finlay Wallace's role within it."

"Are ye thinking what I'm thinking?" Dalgleish cocked his head.

"That our history society was a front for more sinister dealings?" The DI nodded. "Aye, I am. I want every historical stone turned, every record scrutinised. We owe it to Stella, to Lachlan, to Fergus Murray, and even our own Sue."

Helen McAllister nodded. "This murderer likely wants these connections buried once and for all. So, let's expose them."

The DI sighed. "But we are still no further forward with knowing who wants this buried, or having the identities of the two unknowns in the photo. Except..." He frowned. "One of them reminds me of someone. I feel like I've seen him before. I just can't think where."

"Recently?" Dalgleish raised both brows. "Both those men have to be mid- to late-forties in that photo. That would make them more than one hundred years old."

"It wouldn't have been in the flesh. It would have been in a book or photograph."

"You mean the picture you saw that was like this one in Stella's office?"

"No." Grant shook his head. "Leave it with me. It'll come back. Also, we need to locate that other photograph I found in Stella's office. Nothing had been written on the back of it, as I recall, but there may have been accompanying notes in the file."

"I can get onto that, if you let me know where exactly you saw it." Helen nodded.

16

WHERE IS PIERRE?

McKenzie had almost finished his interim report for the DCI when Helen approached his desk, waiting for him to look up.

"Hey, how's it going?" he asked, leaning back in his chair, glad of the respite from writing a draft he hoped would be palatable to Sinclair.

"It's coming on," she answered. "I thought you should know, there's a rumour circulating in online book circles that the Whitlock Tome was sold at a clandestine auction recently."

"Really?" He frowned, sitting upright. "When? Where? Who bought it?"

"No-one is saying when or where, but at least two people have said the buyer's name was Fontaine."

"Fontaine? Could that be Pierre?"

"That was my first thought, sir, yes."

"How reliable is that information?"

"We only have two sources, but they appear to be distinct sources. I couldn't find a connection between the two, apart from the discussion on the online forum. There were at least ten participants in that thread."

McKenzie's pupils enlarged. "I'll bet that auction was here in Edinburgh, and I'll bet that's why Fontaine was here in the first place. I wonder if he already knew his origins, and wanted that book in order to find out more, and use it to locate any inheritance."

Helen nodded. "Perhaps he found out Lachlan Camp-bell had the book and had him killed, or he murdered the bookkeeper himself."

Grant exhaled. "Could he have been behind everything that's happened? It's a leap, but if those rumours were true, then maybe Fontaine knew more than he was letting on all along. His frequent business trips to London and Edinburgh could simply have been a cover. He may have meticulously planned the whole thing."

"Right." She nodded. "So what next? We hunt him down? Find out if he is still here in Edinburgh?"

"Aye, that's exactly what we do. Every second counts, and we don't know what he will do next, or what extremes he is capable of. We have three deaths already, and an attack on one of our own. We want no more murders. If he is busy silencing people, then God only knows who might be next. Let's get everyone together, and we can decide our next moves."

"I'll get the team to the briefing room."

"Thanks, Helen." He stood, crossing over to stare out of the window while he thought through this latest develop-ment. Fontaine had betrayed not a flicker when they told him who his great-great-grandfather was. Except, he hadn't outright denied knowing anything, just appeared surprised. Grant had previously had suspicions about him, but put them on the back burner. There was nothing to connect Pierre to either the murders, or the strange insignia they had found belonging to the mysterious history society in Edinburgh. What had they been missing?

LEITH STATION BRIEFING room quietened down, as the Major Investigation Team, notepads and pens at the ready, awaited instruction from the DI.

"Okay, everyone, thanks for coming." McKenzie addressed officers from both MIT and uniform.

Shirt sleeves rolled up, he ran a hand through his hair. "It appears as though the Whitlock book has resurfaced. If the online conversations Helen has seen are correct, someone called Fontaine bought it in a secret auction. We think it likely this was Pierre Fontaine, a descendant of David Whitlock. We don't have independent confirmation of this, or where this supposed auction happened. But, if it did, there is the possibility that it happened here in Edinburgh, perhaps shortly after Lachlan Campbell's murder. I'll let Helen tell you more."

The DC cleared her throat. "These conversations appeared two weeks ago on a thread discussing the Whitlock book and the rumours going around about it having resurfaced. Two of the participants alleged the book was sold in an underground auction. I have messaged both of them for more information, and their IP addresses and identities are being investigated by our technicians. But, if the rumours are true, it seems the buyer was a Fontaine. I don't yet know if this is our Pierre Fontaine, or a relation, but the possibility is there to be investigated."

McKenzie took over, scanning the faces of his team, each brow furrowing as they absorbed the information. "If Fontaine is still in Edinburgh, I want to speak to him. If he is the killer, and is cleaning up, there could be others in the firing line. Not least, anyone who took part in that auction. Time is not on our side." He paused, allowing the weight of his words to settle. "Someone is busy taking people out. I want him stopped. And, if Fontaine is still in Edinburgh, I want him brought in for questioning. If he is back in France, we will liaise with French colleagues and interview him there."

The mood in the room had sobered, each officer acutely aware they were entering an intense phase.

"We can't wait for our techs to confirm identities. We need to act now if we are to save lives. If we're wrong, I will take the flack," McKenzie continued, "but I want every hotel contacted until we find him. And I want all uniformed units to be alert for him. I trust each of you to do what's necessary."

As the teams dispersed, McKenzie lingered, in two minds whether to hand his report in to Sinclair or wait until Fontaine had been located. "Helen," McKenzie called, as the DC was about to leave, "Thank you. That was a good catch. I know how much work you put into the online searches."

"Thanks. No problem." She smiled. "Let's hope the information was right."

He nodded. "Dig up everything you can on the clandestine auction. We need to know where it was, who was there, who ran it, and prove Pierre Fontaine's link to it."

"Already on it." She grinned, her thin-framed glasses glinting in the overhead lights. "No flies on me."

~

"ANY LUCK?" McKenzie asked Helen as she put the phone down for the umpteenth time. He could see from her expression that she had once again suffered disappointment.

"Nothing."

"How many hotels is that?"

"Eight, so far." Helen sighed. "You know, he could be at an Airbnb. I'll contact the French equivalents of Booking dot com, see if any of them know where he is."

McKenzie shook his head. "If he was off to a secret auction, knowing he was going to silence people along the way, I doubt very much he would have organised his trip through a company. No, he will have privately booked this one, very much a hush hush trip."

"He might have asked the hotel not to speak to us."

"No, I doubt he would do that, either. He won't have wanted to raise the suspicions of the hotel staff. Asking them to not talk to us could have resulted in exactly the opposite, and drawn attention to himself. Whoever killed our victims is far too clever to draw suspicion of any sort. I think he is lying low."

The incessant ring of the telephone cut through their conversation. The DI snatched at the receiver. "Yes?"

"It's front desk. We've received a call from a Louise Fontaine. She says she is the sister of one Pierre Fontaine, and that he is missing. She is really concerned as the family hasn't heard from him in over a week, and she says that isn't like him. We are the third station she has contacted."

"Louise Fontaine?" McKenzie's brow furrowed. "Put her through, please."

"Madame Fontaine?" he asked when he heard her take the phone.

"Mademoiselle Fontaine," she answered in a tremulous voice, with a heavy French accent, and the weariness of one who has been awake most of the night. "But just Louise is fine. I am the sister of Pierre Fontaine. I need you to find him. He hasn't contacted us for eight days. I think something has happened. I phoned his hotel, but they said he hasn't slept in his bed for a week. They did not know whether to keep his room open. They said he has left clothes and toiletries there, but his coat and bag are missing."

He could hear the barely restrained panic in her voice, a sibling grappling with fear and uncertainty.

"Mademoiselle Fontaine, Louise, thank you for calling us. We are also looking for your brother. We saw him eight days ago, and can confirm he was okay then." Grant assured her, his tone deliberately calm, attempting to infuse hope into her bleak situation. "He came in to speak to us about a case we are currently investigating. We have not seen him since, but have received no information to suggest he has been harmed. Can you tell us the name of the hotel? I understand your concern, and I assure you, finding Pierre will be our top priority."

"Merci, monsieur," she replied, blowing her nose. "The hotel is called The Balmoral, in Princes Street. Please find him. This is not like my brother. He texts me or our mother every day. And we have heard nothing from him. He isn't answering his phone. We are so worried."

"I understand, and we will do everything in our power to find him. Can I have your number, please? And your brother's mobile number?"

She reeled off both numbers for him, along with her mother's, for good measure.

McKenzie scribbled them down, ending the call with a promise to keep her informed. His thoughts churned. Was Pierre a perpetrator or victim? What on earth was going on? He filled everyone in regarding Fontaine's last known whereabouts, and telephoned the hotel to let them know they would come to question the staff, and look at the suite in which he had been staying.

The Balmoral Hotel was an iconic five-star establishment in the heart of Edinburgh, and a two-minute walk from Waverley Station.

Dalgleish and McAllister requested CCTV footage from the hotel and surrounding streets, and footage and ticket information from Waverley, hoping to get a handle on where Pierre might have gone, if he had left under his own steam.

McKenzie filled in the DCI before grabbing his jacket and notes, ready to head to the hotel.

"Where's the report I asked you for?" Sinclair glared at him. "You promised me it two days ago. What's going on?"

"I'm not sure, sir," he answered. "We have a suspect for the murders, but his sister reported him missing," he answered. "We are on it, though, and hope to have located him by the end of the day."

"What do you mean, he is missing? Has he gone underground?"

"Not sure, yet. But, like I say, we should have an update for you later. I'm off to his last known whereabouts now, sir. The Balmoral Hotel. If he has gone underground, we hope to locate him via the City's CCTV, and pinging his mobile. Dalgleish and McAllister are on it."

"How is Susan?" Sinclair pushed his hands into his trouser pockets.

"She doing well. I saw her yesterday. She is in good spirits, though couldn't tell us much about her attacker. One thing we are sure of, however, is the link between that attack and our case. We are all being extra cautious now, sir, and Sue's partner Greg has taken some time off work to be with her at home until she comes back to work next week. He is a highly skilled officer. If anyone can keep her safe, he can."

"Right." Sinclair nodded. "Keep me informed. Don't leave me in the dark for days again."

"I will. I mean, I won't. Oh..."

Sinclair laughed. "Go on, get on with it."

"Right." McKenzie closed the door behind him

"Grant?" Helen called over to him, her eyes grave. "We've been checking the CCTV we've collected so far, particularly around Waverley station, in case Fontaine took a trip somewhere."

"And?" He pinched the bridge of his nose to fend off a headache. So far, it wasn't working.

"Surveillance systems were down at Waverley Station eight days ago, and the footage from the last two days has become corrupted. It's set us back; we can't track movements during the crucial window when Pierre went missing."

"Damn it," McKenzie cursed under his breath. "What about the street cameras and shops?"

"Graham is going through all that has come in so far. It'll take us a while, though. With Sue out of action, things are taking us a little longer. Do you need someone to go with you to The Balmoral?"

He shook his head. "You will be more useful here. If I suspect anything untoward has gone on at the hotel, I'll get forensics in. You guys continue what you are doing, and I'll give you a bell later to let you know how I get on."

"Will do," she nodded. "Leave it with us."

"Thanks, Helen." He grabbed his coat, feeling lucky to have a team that would so willingly pull out all the stops, as they did so often. But he couldn't shake the gnawing fear they were all one step behind a killer who still lurked unseen — a phantom. The hunt for Pierre Fontaine was now a race against time. And the clock was ticking.

17

THE EMPTY HOTEL ROOM

The Balmoral Hotel sported a grand, marbled lobby, with high ceilings and intricate mouldings, reflecting the building's historic past. Elaborate chandeliers, plush-fabric seating, and fresh flowers mixed traditional Scottish comfort with a contemporary feel.

The hotel also boasted the Michelin-starred restaurant Number One, offering fine dining, and the Scotch Whisky Bar, boasting one of Scotland's largest collections of single malts. The DI had never stayed there himself, but he had visited when he had cause through work. These occasions, however, had never involved tasting or imbibing the mouth-watering things on offer.

Pierre Fontaine had chosen a deluxe suite with a spacious, elegantly appointed room for his stay, which was to have been for one month. He had overstayed this by several days, which was why the hotel wanted the room vacated. McKenzie checked the hotel register, noting the times Fontaine had checked in and out, the last time being eight days previous.

A porter showed McKenzie to the Frenchman's room,

hovering by the door until the DI explained he would prefer examining the suite alone.

He had entered a large room with a king-sized bed, adorned with top-notch linens and perfectly plump pillows. The amenities included a work desk with ergonomic seating, high-speed Wi-Fi, and multiple charging points for electronic devices. The arrangement evidently catered to business executives. Pierre's suit and a few other pieces of clothing hung in the wardrobe, and an antique-hunter's magazine lay on the bedside cabinet. If Fontaine had helped himself to the complimentary bar, the tiny bottles had since been replaced.

The living area, furnished with comfortable sofas, a flat-screen TV, and a selection of fine art that would have appealed to the art and antiques collector, offered stunning views of Edinburgh Castle through the floor-to-ceiling window. A metal case with wheels and an extendable handle stood in one corner of the room. The DI put on latex gloved to examine it. It was empty, even the pockets.

The marble bathroom, featuring a deep tub and walk-in shower, contained toiletries from Penhaligon's. But, aside from his expensive wash-bag and razor, the DI would not have known Fontaine had been there. All the towels and toiletries were fresh and unused; replaced daily, despite the occupier's absence.

The manager had earlier explained that Pierre used the hotel's spa and fitness centre several times during his stay, and had always been polite and friendly to staff and other guests alike. So far, he didn't sound like a serial killer. But appearances could be deceptive.

McKenzie sifted through drawers, but found only Fontaine's briefs, fountain pen and ink, tee-shirts, and a pair of lounge pants. There were no other personal effects. If he had brought a laptop, he had taken it with him, along with his mobile phone and wallet.

The DI phoned the office.

"Found anything?" Dalgleish asked.

"No, nothing." He answered with a sigh. "It's like he vanished into thin air, leaving no clues to where he has gone. There is no notebook here, nothing. What about you? What is CCTV revealing?"

"Nothing so far, I'm afraid. We are still going through hotel footage. We have him in the lobby a few times on the day he disappeared, but nothing of him leaving yet."

"Keep looking," McKenzie instructed, eyes sweeping the room. "I'm almost done here. I'll be heading back shortly."

As McKenzie left The Balmoral Hotel, a sense of unease settled in his stomach, the kind that gnawed away at him when cases took a turn for the worse.

"We need to expand the search," he said as he walked into the office. "Check CCTV from the surrounding areas, talk to local businesses, get uniform canvassing the streets. We can employ facial recognition software on city-wide CCTV. I want traffic cameras, ATMs, public transport, and anything else that might have glimpsed Fontaine."

"On it." Dalgleish nodded.

The DI stood, hands on hips, studying a whiteboard littered with leads and dead ends. His mind raced. "We need to think outside the box," he muttered.

Graham tapped on his laptop. "I'll coordinate with technicians, pull in favours if I must. We can cross-reference timeframes with his last known movements."

"Aye, good." McKenzie turned to McAllister, who was

halfway out the door, "Helen, reach out to our informants. Find out if they heard anything about the auction or the French businessman."

"Got ya."

The team got on with things, leaving McKenzie deep in thought. Could Pierre Fontaine, the great-great-grandson of David Whitlock, be in danger? The thought pricked at him like thistles from the Cairngorms. Something about this whole situation felt off.

GRANT'S unmarked car rolled to a stop near Stella MacLeod's office. He sat contemplating for a moment, gaze fixed on the weathered sign above the door; mind ticking over the disparate pieces of information he was holding in his head. The memory tugging at him concerned the photograph of the Nazi Dieter Schmidt at the clandestine meeting during the Second World War, in which he thought he recognised a face among the participants, but couldn't place it. He had been turning this over in his mind since the early hours, as it teased the edges of his consciousness, robbing him of sleep. But he had an idea and was about to check it out.

He strode to the door, eyes scanning the now vacant office. Though forensic officers had long since finished their examination of it, their torn tape still clung to the door. McKenzie pushed it aside and tried the handle. It was locked. Someone had sellotaped a note to the letterbox, advising that they had left the key at a neighbouring shop. The DI knew the shop and its owner, Aileen.

The bell above the door chimed a greeting that was almost too cheerful for the business at hand. "Morning,

Aileen," he called, tone jovial despite his brain feeling mashed.

"Grant, you're looking dour." Well-fed and forty, Aileen grinned, her keen eyes missing nothing as she emerged from the rows of shelves filled with trinkets and tartans. "What brings ye here?"

"Och, I need the keys for another look around the office next door," he shrugged. "I always like to have one last look, in case we missed anything."

"Aye, that was a terrible business…" She leaned over the counter conspiratorially. "Do ye ken who did it?"

"The key, if you don't mind." He gave her a mock scolding look.

"I'll go get it." She tutted. "You never give anything away, you."

She fetched the key from a hook beneath the counter, offering it with a solemn nod. Her fingers lingered on the cool metal as her eyes clouded over. "I'll miss her, you know, giving me a wave in the morning…" She shook her head. "I wish I'd known her better."

"Aye, she kept herself to herself." McKenzie nodded. "You have a good day now, you hear?"

"Aye, I'll try."

RETURNING TO THE OFFICE, he unlocked the door, stepping inside the hush that had enveloped the building. The familiar scent of old books and dust greeted him, a reminder of the woman who had once worked here. Every corner whispered of her, and of the historic stories she had kept and archived with true diligence.

His gaze swept the room, coming to rest on the

mahogany bookcases that stood silently watching over it. He could see her standing there, fingers tracing book spines with absent-minded reverence, before drawing out that lever-arch file — the one he now sought. The one from which she had photocopied the notes she gave to them.

He found it again, pulling it from the shelf before settling into Stella's chair, the place she would occupy herself if she had still been there.

Grant opened it, scanning page after page, till his eyes were sore.

"Come on, Stella lass," he murmured. "Help me out here."

Finally, his patience was rewarded.

As he flicked through the historian's meticulous collection, he found it. The photograph, its edges worn from time and handling. A faded black-and-white image turned sepia with age, revealing two young men clad in the unmistakable officer uniforms of World War I. Their expressions stoic, and shaped by the solemnity of their duty. David Whitlock and Quentin Hugh-Wynstanley stood shoulder to shoulder, immortalised in the moments before setting off back to a war that would carve deep lines and scars into European lands, and the hearts of loved ones left behind.

McKenzie knew at once this was a copy of the photograph he had seen lodged in the archives at Winston Hall, belonging to Quentin Hugh-Wynstanley's descendants.

As he held the photograph, eyes lingering on the faces of the two young men who had been best friends since children, a grim recognition washed over him; a connection resurfacing in his mind. A jigsaw piece fell into place in his head. The photo they had discovered at Stella's home, taken at the covert meeting with Dieter Schmidt during the Second World War, now made harrowing sense. The face he had recognised was that of David's best friend, Quentin. It was Quentin Hugh-Wynstanley at that meeting with Dieter Schmidt, decades after the sepia photograph in his hands was taken.

Turning his attention back to the file, he continued rifling through the pages, pausing only to read Stella's notes in the margin.

One caught his eye, and he squinted at the faded ink, piecing together the cryptic remarks framing the text. A silent dialogue between Stella and herself, that he was now party to. But what was she saying?

As he deciphered the scrawled script, one name stood out, Fergus Murray. It was dated the day before someone knocked Murray off his bike and killed him. The historian had briefly noted a discussion she had with the geocacher, but not what the conversation was about.

The DI ran a hand through his hair. Why did everything to do with this case feel like pulling teeth? He couldn't remember the last time the witnesses in an investigation had seemed so closed off and secretive.

He continued reading. Another margin note said simply, 'Network — The Keepers'. Stella had written the words, followed by dates that straddled the two global conflicts. He was still struggling to figure out the significance of this when his blood ran cold. There, near the bottom of the page, was an image of the insignia he had seen carved next to Lachlan Campbell's body; the one whose meaning they had been seeking since they found him. It appeared along with another photograph taken at the nineteen-forties get-together with Dieter Schmidt.

"Christ!" He rubbed his forehead, the room contracting around him. 'Wealth through treachery,' the historian had written, next to the circled face of Quentin Hugh-Wynstanley.

What did Quentin do? Grant frowned.

There was a line he couldn't make out, followed by the word, 'Treason.' Had Hugh-Wynstanley accepted blood money? McKenzie's hand trembled as he traced the words, realising the potential significance. Stiff-jawed, his narrowed eyes examined the photographs again. Quentin Hugh-Wynstanley was a spy. David Whitlock's closest friend and confidant had been a traitor. At least, it looked as though Stella thought so. But was she right? And did the T.K. in the insignia represent 'The Keepers', as per Stella's margin note?"

"Bloody hell..." McKenzie closed the file with a thud. Pieces of the puzzle were falling into place. He pondered this new information, the potential implications were sobering, and may have dictated events over decades, linking the dead and the living in a chain of deceit that had ensnared more than the men standing shoulder-to-shoulder in the photograph with the Nazi.

He tucked the file under his arm, and headed back to his car, giving a wave to Aileen McPherson who was standing in the glass doorway of her shop, still watching to see what he was up to.

18

AN UNEXPECTED KIDNAP

McKenzie phoned Dalgleish.

"Grant? Where are you? Are you till at Stella's?"

"Aye, I'm just leaving," he answered, sounding breathless. "I found photos and notes in her office archives that suggest a spy network, linked to the Hugh-Wynstanleys, was operating for decades. I don't know all the ins and outs, I only know that Stella was researching this stuff, and it was probably what she was going to discuss with me before someone took her out. It could explain why someone murdered her and burgled her office. I think her research may have been what the killer was looking for, if not the Whitlock book."

Dalgleish whistled through his teeth. "So why wasn't the file taken during the break-in?"

"The dates."

"What?"

"I didn't read the label when she showed us the file in the office. I only remembered roughly where on the shelf she had put it. But the label on it says, 'Edinburgh during the plague'. Perhaps it was euphemism, but I think she knew that title would not attract attention from whoever she was frightened of. Whoever broke into her office had no interest in a file from that era. But inside, the contents were all about the Whitlocks, and the World Wars, and the research Stella had been doing, making notes alluding to betrayals. It looks like Quentin Hugh-Wynstanley was making money selling secrets, and the fake history society he set up was still up to no good, thirty years later. Likely, still selling information."

"Christ!"

"Exactly..." The DI continued. "God only knows how much of that family's wealth they owe to treasonous activities. But I want you to organise a formal interview with the heirs. Tell them we want to speak to them again, but do not tell them why, at this stage. This could be the break in the case we've been looking for."

"Understood, sir," Graham replied. "We'll have everything prepped. Be careful out there."

"Always am," McKenzie replied.

The DC cleared his throat. "By the way, Susan is back."

"Is she?" The DI frowned. "Is she well enough to be in?"

"She says she is, but we are making sure she's not doing too much."

"Good... Tell her I will be there shortly. Thanks, Graham." He ended the call, slipping the phone back into his coat pocket, his mind already considering their next moves in this deadly investigation. He felt the weight of the case pressing down on him like the heavy Leith fog. The air was thick with the promise of rain, the ominous clouds mirroring the dark path the case seemed to be taking.

As he walked to his car, along a now busy street, wary of puddles on the damp pavement, McKenzie thought of Rosemary Whitlock and her book. Had she known of Quentin's treachery? Is that why some of her letters to him seemed pointed? Barbed, even? Was that man the reason she feared someone would shoot her husband in the back? "We're getting closer, Rosemary," he murmured, his words drowned out by shoppers and traffic. But, although the fog around their inquiry was steadily clearing, dark clouds seemed ever more palpable. Somewhere out there, a murderer watched and waited, killing from the shadows. The DI was determined to drag them out into the light.

He slid behind the wheel of his unmarked car, head full of the case, as he drove back to Leith station. The killer or killers had played their hand well, but Stella Macleod had outwitted them, even in death, and McKenzie was determined to finish what the canny historian had started.

THE SIGHTS of Edinburgh blurred past McKenzie's window as he steered through the city's veins.

A thought struck him, sharp and unwelcome, like his alarm clock that morning, waking him from a dream he had been enjoying. If the Hugh-Wynstanleys were suspect number one, what of Pierre Fontaine, the antique art collector, writer, and David Whitlock's living legacy? If he wasn't the perpetrator, or in league with the perpetrators, did that mean he was potentially a victim? Perhaps Fontaine had not simply chosen to disappear. Maybe something worse had befallen him.

"Damn it," the DI cursed under his breath, knuckles whitening on the steering wheel, as anxiety gnawed at his gut. Perhaps Fontaine, in his quest for art antiques, and maybe his ancestor's biography, had fallen foul of the killers plaguing all those connected to the Whitlock Tome.

He flicked on his indicator, taking a swift left turn down a narrow street. Eyes scanning the rear-view mirror, searching for any sign of a tail. The killer had attacked Susan Robertson. All in his team were now hyper-vigilant.

"Fontaine doesn't know what he's tangled up in," he muttered. "I hope we locate him before he finds out."

DALGLEISH CAUGHT McKenzie as soon as he arrived back, tie loose, sleeves rolled up, and rubbing the back of his neck.

"What's happened?" The DI's eyes narrowed.

"It's Pierre Fontaine. I think someone may have kidnapped him."

"Go on..."

"I have him on CCTV footage from the cameras near a cafe in Edinburgh's Old Town, on the day he disappeared," Dalgleish began, his throat tight with tension. "He got into the back of a Silver BMW. The car raced away at speed."

Grant's eyes narrowed. "A silver BMW? He asked, thinking of the car that was seen near Lachlan Campbell's address by his cleaner. Do we have a license plate?"

Dalgleish shook his head. "Not from that camera. There were vehicles behind, blocking the view. But how the car pulled away gives me a bad feeling, I can tell you. Take a look for yourself." He crossed over to his laptop. "See this?" he asked. "Watch this bit here..." He pointed at the Silver BMW coming into frame.

The DI's brow furrowed in concentration.

On the monitor, Pierre Fontaine's figure emerged from the cafe, a courier bag over his shoulder. He spoke to through the window of the car, before someone swung open a door of the vehicle and pulled him into the back seat. The car lurched forward, peeling off into the traffic. And then it was gone, leaving nothing but an Edinburgh street going about its daily business.

"Damn it!" McKenzie muttered under his breath, rubbing a hand across his beard. He felt his gut clench. "That doesn't look like a willing departure to me."

"I didn't think so either," Dalgleish agreed. "But there's more... I haven't been able to get a response from the Hugh-Wynstanleys. I've tried calling them several times, to arrange an interview like you asked. Either they are not at their home, or they are choosing not to answer the phone."

Grant frowned. "I bet they have a silver BMW. And, if they have Pierre, either he is involved in whatever is going on, or he does not know what he is getting involved in. Either way, we need to find him, and fast."

He strode back to his desk, snatching up the phone, and punching in the number for Winston Hall. The dial tone droned on, but the phone remained unanswered. Grant slammed the receiver down and pondered their next move.

"Still no answer?" McAllister asked, walking over to him.

"Nothing," McKenzie confirmed, a muscle jumping in his jaw. "Either they are ignoring all calls, or they are not there."

"Our calls will read 'no number' on their phone. Could be they are concerned about calls from us." Dalgleish shrugged. "Or you are right, they are not there. Either way, I think we shouldn't leave anything to chance."

"Exactly." McKenzie nodded. "We're wasting time. We have the direction they were heading, don't we?"

"We do." Dalgleish nodded. "We think we have the car

again on footage from several other cameras, heading out of the city on the A7."

McKenzie frowned. "If the Hugh-Wynstanleys have taken him, that is the route they would have gone. A7 to A720, and then onto the A1, just as we did when we travelled to Yorkshire. I'll bet they are taking our Pierre Fontaine to Winston Hall. Maybe they think he knows where the Whitlock Tome is. They would consider that book a risk to their inheritance. That could be motive enough for murder."

"Well, if Pierre knows where Rosemary's book is, let's hope he hasn't told them. There's nothing to stop them from killing him if they have the book."

Grant stood up, mind racing. "Exactly. If he has talked, he may already be dead." He picked up the phone once more and dialled the number for the West Yorkshire police.

AFTER A TENSE FEW MOMENTS, he connected to DCI Keith Cummings. "Sorry to bother you, sir, it's DI McKenzie from MIT, Edinburgh. We've got a situation. We believe a visitor to our city has been kidnapped and transported to Winston Hall in Yorkshire. His name is Pierre Fontaine, and we suspect Horatio and William Hugh-Wynstanley of taking him. He might still be at Winston Hall. No-one has heard from him for nine days. We've been investigating a string of murders in the city, and all roads are currently leading us to the Hugh-Wynstanleys. I will speak to our DCI, Rob Sinclair, who will contact you shortly, but I have only just received this news and thought we should act on it."

"What are you suggesting?" Cummings asked. "Do you need an armed division to attend? And how sure are you that a kidnap has taken place? The Hugh-Wynstanleys are a prominent family here."

"We're fairly sure, sir. And we fear for his safety. To be frank, sir, he may even already be dead."

"Right," came the curt response. "What do you need?"

"I think an armed response team would be the best option at this point. If I am wrong, I apologise, but we believe the danger is real. We haven't been able to ping his phone since the day he disappeared. But he didn't leave it in his hotel room. If your guys could surround the house with armed officers and try to communicate with those inside. We'll be on our way as soon as I have informed our DCI."

Cummings' voice was calm but firm. "Understood, McKenzie. We'll handle it from here. Tell Rob to call me as soon as soon as he can and get someone to email the details of what has gone on as soon as possible."

"Aye, I will do, sir." Grant hung up and turned to Dalgleish. "Get everyone ready to head up there. I've got to have a quick word with the DCI. Would you be able to email some details over to DCI Cummings in West Yorkshire while I am with Sinclair?"

"No problem." Dalgleish nodded.

"Thanks, Graham. As soon as I have spoken to Rob, we'll head over to Yorkshire."

19

STAND-OFF

M cKenzie exited Sinclair's office, eyes scanning the faces of his team. "Okay, listen up... We're heading to Winston Hall, as we believe that's where they have taken Fontaine. Forensic officers are combing through his room for any additional clues, but I want eyes on that Yorkshire mansion. The Hugh-Wynstan-leys are our now our prime suspects, and we need to move before they get wind we're onto them."

McAllister nodded, her voice steady despite the unease. "What's our approach?"

"We go full tilt," the DI answered. "West Yorkshire is heading up the operation for now. But remember, kidnapping is not murder. If the Hugh-Wynstanleys are our killers, Pierre must have something they want. Maybe the Whitlock Tome. But, if they're desperate enough to grab him, they are obviously willing to risk everything, and that makes them dangerous both to Fontaine, and us."

His gaze swept over his team, each member taut and ready. "All right, gear up. We leave in five."

The unit sprang into action, the clatter of equipment

and murmur of voices, in stark contrast to the silent tension moments before. McKenzie watched them, pride mingled with concern. This was a different game, and the stakes had never been higher.

MINUTES LATER, they were barreling down the A1 towards Yorkshire, the hum of the engine blending with the occasional siren as they weaved in and out of traffic. The countryside flashed by in a blur, McKenzie remaining focussed as his mind ran through scenarios, hoping Fontaine was still alive.

Everyone held their breath for long periods. Grant, Graham, Helen, and a stubborn Susan, who had refused to stay back at the office, rode in silence now, each lost in their thoughts, hoping they would get there on time. Grant pressed as hard on the accelerator as the speed limits and traffic allowed.

"ETA twenty minutes, sir," Dalgleish confirmed.

"Good." The DI checked his watch. Rain began spattering the windshield, the droplets racing one another across the glass, driven by the rush of air over the vehicle.

Chatter came over Dalgleish's radio.

"Anything from the negotiations team?" McKenzie asked.

"They are at the Hall, sir. It sounds like they are all in position."

"Good. That's something, at least." He exhaled. "We need eyes on Fontaine."

As THEY APPROACHED WINSTON HALL, a flurry of police activity greeted them. West Yorkshire police had surrounded the grand estate, their vehicles creating a perimeter around the imposing stone mansion. Armed officers positioned themselves strategically around the home and outbuildings, and a negotiator was speaking to those inside through a megaphone.

The wheels of their unmarked vehicle crunched over gravel as it came to a halt on the tree-lined route to Winston Hall's imposing iron gates. Grant parked the car at a slant, and all four detectives hurried to the command post.

The DI introduced himself to the police sergeant standing guard. "DI McKenzie, Leith MIT. We've been tracking this case from Edinburgh."

"They're refusing to let our negotiator in," the sergeant briefed in hushed tones. "They're claiming they have a hostage."

"Got any visuals on the hostage?" McKenzie asked, his piercing blue eyes scanning every visible window for movement.

"Not yet, I'm afraid. Cameras only show the exterior," he replied. "That's the DCI approaching. He'll know more." The sergeant turned his attention back to the house.

DCI Cummings greeted them with a nod, lips pressed into a thin line. "We've made contact. The brothers, Horatio and William, are inside, along with their father. They tell us he is unwell, and that all this activity is frightening him. They denied having Fontaine there at first, but they now tell us they have him as hostage. The silver BMW, seen on CCTV, has been parked at the side of the mansion. We have asked the brothers to come and speak to us, and show us the hostage, but they have so far refused to cooperate. So we don't yet know whether Fontaine is still alive."

McKenzie nodded, feeling unusually small beside the Yorkshire DCI. The man had to be Six-foot-five. "They have to come to the door." Grant looked towards the house, scanning the windows, unable to see anyone. He clenched his fists. "I wish we could get in there."

Cummings shook his head. "We must be cautious, as they are likely armed, and you say you suspect they have already killed others. Rushing in could be a risk to your man, Fontaine."

"I agree with you, sir. This should be handled carefully. No sudden moves. If these men are our killers, they have murdered three times before. And I believe, they won't hesitate to do so again."

THE STANDOFF at Winston Hall had been going on for over two hours. Mckenzie mopped perspiration from his forehead in the humid air of an approaching storm. He watched as the Yorkshire police negotiator worked on the men inside, her voice alternating between soothing and commanding, as she spoke through the megaphone. Officers in full gear, with machine guns, added the threat of deadly force, should it prove necessary. All this had put the men inside on edge.

"Horatio, William," the negotiator called, "you have nowhere to go. Let's end this peacefully, before anyone gets hurt."

Shadows flickered across the grand windows as the Hugh-Wynstanley brothers paced, desperation increasing as their options dwindled. But the officers acted with patience, with a hostage's life on the line.

"Sir, thermal monitors are showing increased movement," DC Dalgleish reported, his voice low in McKenzie's ear. "I think something is about to happen."

The DI nodded, acknowledging the update with tense shoulders.

"Hold the line," Cummings instructed tersely. His words met with affirmations over the radio from his team.

Suddenly, a side door on the manor burst open.

Horatio and William emerged, erratic and frenzied, and pushing a terrified Pierre Fontaine who cowered in front of them.

"Stay back!" William ordered the waiting officers. "We'll kill him."

"Damn it..." McKenzie cursed under his breath as he watched the brothers pulling at Fontaine in their attempt to manoeuvre him around the side of the mansion, where the BMW sat.

As the West Yorkshire team silently moved to new positions, thunder rent the sky, and rain began pounding the ground around them.

"Stay calm," Grant muttered. "Don't rush this."

The spatter of raindrops on men and equipment was barely audible over the tense communication and radio chatter. From his new vantage point behind a column, DI McKenzie observed the West Yorkshire police negotiator attempting to reason with Horatio and William. Armed officers observed the brothers on the East side of Winston Hall. William held a large kitchen knife to Pierre Fontaine's throat.

Near the hall, the negotiator held up a hand. "We need more time," she said. "We can't give you immunity... A helicopter can be here, just not that quickly."

"Get one here, now!" Horatio ordered, his voice high-pitched. "Or we'll kill him."

McKenzie clenched his fists, knuckles white with frustration.

"Diversion team, are you ready?" Cummings came over his earpiece.

"Affirmative, sir," came the response. "We're set up and ready to go on your signal."

"Good. Standby."

McKenzie took a deep breath, looking across at Dalgleish. "They are getting ready to move."

"Understood." Graham nodded.

"Go, go, go!" Cummings directed

McKenzie and his team watched as another group of armed officers came from around the back of the building, taking the Hugh-Wynstanley brothers by surprise. Now, they had officers to their front and rear, and could not use Fontaine as a shield from both.

Negotiations were no longer an option.

With a guttural scream, Horatio pushed Fontaine to the ground as he and William made a run for the BMW parked at the side of the house.

"For god's sake, go!" McKenzie barked out loud. "We canna let them get away!"

As though responding to his words, shots rang out from the armed officers. The tyres on the BMW deflated, and several rounds pierced the car's doors.

William stopped dead, putting his hands up, shortly followed by Horatio.

Rain poured down relentlessly, drenching the officers and captives, as the men from West Yorkshire handcuffed the brothers.

Grant turned to Fontaine, crumpled on the wet ground, shaking uncontrollably. He turned open-mouthed to the DI, as though still unsure what had happened.

"You're safe now, Pierre," he assured him, placing a hand on his shoulder. "We've got you."

"Merci," Fontaine whispered, tears mingling with rain on his cheeks.

"Good work," McKenzie praised West Yorkshire officers as they filed past, removing helmets and heavy gear. They had done it. They had apprehended the culprits and secured Pierre's safety. The relief was palpable.

"Let's get out of this rain." The DI gestured for his team to follow him as armed men escorted the prisoners to waiting police vans.

20

LOST LOVES

The DI's shoes clacked against the cold marble floor as he navigated the labyrinthine corridors of Winston Hall, guided by Pierre. He followed him to the Hugh-Wynstanley archive room, as McAllister and Dalgleish left to check on the brothers' father, Phillip, who was being checked over by paramedics from the ambulances which had been on standby.

Grant turned to Fontaine. "Pierre, do you need medical attention? I really think you ought to be checked over."

He turned to him, appearing calm and less shaky than he had only thirty minutes before. "I'm not harmed. I'll be all right. But, you must see this..." He led the detective down the hall to the archive room, and to a thick, gilded volume lying on a table. "This... This is it," he said, picking up the tome and handing it to Grant. "This is the book everybody has been searching for. You are holding the only copy ever printed of Rosemary Whitlock's homage to her husband."

It felt almost too precious to touch. The DI felt he ought to be wearing fine, white cotton gloves. The ones worn by historians and archivists looking after the world's most precious relics. It seemed sacrilegious to do otherwise. And yet, here he was, holding this heavy, weathered tome in his bare hands. This book had been sought by collectors and historians world-over for the best part of a century, including the murdered Lachlan Campbell.

McKenzie traced the contours of the binding with his fingers, swallowing hard as he opened up the front cover. There, in faded blue fountain pen ink, underneath the dedication, was a paragraph handwritten by Rosemary Whitlock herself.

JUNE, 1918.

To my darling husband, David.

The last four years have felt like four decades. I pray with all my heart that you are keeping safe, and that the war ends soon. The book I have just now finished, I wrote with you and your safety in mind, my love. I hope you will read it on your return from those war-torn fields in France. And I hope I have done you and your family justice within its pages.

My darling, I know you worry about being the last of your line. But, on your return, have faith that we can change that. I know my writing has taken me away from you for long periods, even before you went away. But you are always with me, as I hope you feel me with you, while you face the worst evils humanity has to offer. I am at a loss now, this book being finished. You are still so very far away; facing a peril I can only imagine and despair at. I shall fill my days with letters to you, some sent; some unsent. Keep safe, my darling, until we meet again. I hold you in my heart, always.

All my love,

Rosemary.

UNCHARACTERISTIC TEARS PRICKED HIS EYES. The DI blinked them back as he flipped through the yellowed pages of the Whitlock Tome.

"She wrote it to keep him safe, didn't she?" McKenzie looked up at Pierre, who was watching him from his position near the window.

He nodded. "Yes, I think she did... Lachlan told me, you know, when he loaned me her book. He had carried out extensive research over the years. He knew the Whitlock's story better than his own. But it was only after he possessed the book, and read it, that he knew the full extent of Rosemary's love, and the lengths to which she had gone to ensure her husband's safety. Lachie had worked it out... the treachery of Quentin Hugh-Wynstanley and his family. The clandestine meetings, the passing of secrets, and the vast sums of money changing hands. Rosemary encoded all of it within her book, and held it over Quentin's head, warning him that if anything happened to her husband, she would take everything she knew to the police. The Hugh-Wynstanleys would have lost everything. And Quentin would have faced a firing squad, instead of the hero's welcome and medals he received. Lachie told me all this when we met... when he loaned me Rosemary's book. He sought me out, before I had any idea where I had come from. Of course, I knew who my parents and grandparents were, but there was always a mystery surrounding my great-great-grandfather — a man spoken about in whispers and hushed voices. I never understood until Monsieur Campbell explained it all to me."

"But you knew about your great-great-grandmother, Yvette?"

Fontaine nodded. "Oh yes, I had always known about her. She loved David too, very much. He must have been a special person, albeit one who was flawed. I wonder if he ever felt guilt about cheating on his wife. But I doubt there was enough time to dwell amidst the mayhem of trench warfare."

McKenzie pressed his lips together. "No, perhaps not..."

"I wanted to confront them with what I knew." Pierre shook his head. "I cannot believe I was so foolish as to think I could throw it in their face without consequence. You see, I was so angry when Lachlan died. I was determined to find out if it was they who murdered him. So, I met them. I wanted to do it in a cafe, but they insisted on talking in the car. How could I have been so stupid? Of course, they wouldn't let me walk away after that."

"Why didn't you come to us? Why didn't you tell us any of this? Everything Lachlan told you? You knew we were investigating his murder. You could have helped us end this whole thing sooner. It is an offence in this country to withhold information or interfere with a police investigation."

Fontaine sighed, shoulders hunching over; head bowed. "I had the Whitlock book, and I had been to see Lachlan before he was murdered. I was sure you would think I had killed him. The papers and TV were all speculating that someone had murdered him for the book and had then stolen it. I thought you would think I was responsible. My DNA is likely in that attic room, where I sat at the desk with him. And, like I say, I had Rosemary's book. I was to read it over a period of weeks and then return it to Lachlan. I planned my stay in Edinburgh accordingly." He ran a hand through his hair. "Believe me, I am sorry I went to the brothers first. I thought I could handle myself, but they were stronger. I regretted it every single minute they kept me here in this room."

McKenzie turned towards the door.

"Wait... There's something else." Pierre grabbed an old shoebox, surrounded with brown parcel tape, from the bottom shelf, hidden from prying eyes behind books.

"Are those letters?" McKenzie's eyes narrowed.

"They taunted me with them," Fontaine answered. "They dangled them in front of me while I sat hunched up on the floor over there, my wrists zip-tied."

"I don't understand..."

"Quentin Hugh-Wynstanley stole them from both David Whitlock and, later, Rosemary Whitlock. Lachie told me he believed Quentin killed my great-great-grandfather and took all of his letters, lest any betray the secrets David had uncovered about him. Then, when Hugh-Wynstanley stole Rosemary's book as she lay dying, he also took many of her letters — for the same reason."

"My God..." The DI shook his head. "The man had no heart."

Pierre's hands trembled as he pulled two small stacks from the old shoebox, gently pulling on the ribbons tying first one, then the other.

He plucked the topmost envelope from the pile, addressed in a delicate, faded script. The old letter crackled, disturbed after almost one hundred years of rest. The Frenchman's eyes widened. "This is from my great-great-grandmother, Yvette, to David while he was in the trenches. Written in English," he said, before flicking through more of the envelopes. "There are more from Yvette to David. These must be the ones Quentin stole from him all those years ago."

"May I see?" Grant stepped forward.

"Of course…" Fontaine handed it over, turning his attention to other letters from the pile.

The DI took in the words, each sentence unveiling layers from the lives of people he had only known about through the course of a murder investigation. It was all there, amidst the tender inquiries about health and weather, and mundane details of everyday existence during that awful war, the love they had for each other. A lump formed in the McKenzie's throat.

Pierre continued flicking through the missives, his curiosity an insatiable hunger for truth. "There are letters here from Rosemary to David, too. And these," he said, flicking through the second pile, "are David's letters to his wife." His brows knitted together, casting shadows over eyes that flickered across the pages, and signalled a profound sadness and melancholy for the love that both Rosemary and his great-great-grandmother had lost, and for David, who had loved both of them.

The DI understood, and to an extent, he felt that sadness too. "What a mess," he said.

As McKenzie left Pierre to his examination of the letters, he wondered if he should have stopped him. There would be retrospective investigations of the deaths of both David Whitlock, and Rosemary Whitlock, and those letters seized in evidence. And Fontaine would be called to give his evidence in the trials of both Horatio and William Hugh-Wynstanley, for the deaths of Lachlan Campbell, Stella MacLeod, and Fergus Murray. But the DI had not the heart to stop the Frenchman at that moment from discovering more about his past.

They could take the letters in due course.

21

A WEB OF DECEIT

Leaning against the cool stone wall of Winston Hall, DI McKenzie watched his team liaising with the West Yorkshire officers. He thought, not for the first time, how good they were at their work, and how lucky he was to be their DI. They were so proficient, in fact, he felt like a spare part at times. But he didn't mind. He was sometimes glad of the respite. The last several days had been tense and fraught, and he had an upset stomach to prove it. If he had been a smoker, he would have lit up now. It seemed like an appropriate time to do so. But he wasn't. Instead, he took in a lungful of fresh country air, and thanked providence for the safe release of David Whitlock's heir, Pierre Fontaine.

His gaze lingered on the ancient Whitlock tome, now bagged as evidence, and cradled in Helen McAllister's careful hands.

She saw him looking, and approached, leaving the rest of their team in conversation with the Yorkshire men.

"Can you believe it?" She asked, her voice soft in

empathy with his contemplative silence. "The lengths they went to, taking people out, then hiding the truth in plain sight like that?"

He pursed his lips. "I doubt the letters were in that archive room to begin with. I suspect they moved them there after Graham and I spent hours searching through their documents. They probably believed we'd be unlikely to search there again."

She nodded. "And, finally, we have this." She held up Rosemary's book. "At least now we know it exists, eh? I know you had your doubts."

"I did. Fergus Murray almost had me convinced we were looking for a phantom product of Rosemary's imagination."

"I wonder if he really believed that himself?"

"I don't know..." McKenzie's gaze turned to the fields in the distance. "It's hard to say. Maybe he wanted to put us off the scent. Perhaps he was secretly still looking for it himself. I think the Hugh-Wynstanleys must have suspected him of knowing something, if it was they who killed him?"

"I wonder if they will confess to his murder?"

"If we cannot prove it, I doubt they will." He shook his head. "But time will tell."

"I'd better get this to the car," she said, holding the bagged tome to her chest.

"Treat that book with great care," McKenzie replied. "We wouldn't want to be responsible for it disappearing again." He gave her a wry smile, before turning to face the rest of his team, taking in the fatigue etched on their furrowed foreheads, a weariness he shared after the previous few weeks.

"You all did great work," he smiled, his eyes meeting each of theirs. "This wasn't only about catching killers. It was about restoring peace to souls long-since passed."

"Rosemary Whitlock would be proud, eh?" Graham loosened his tie, unbuttoning the top button of his shirt in the heat from the strong early-afternoon sun that had cleared away most of the cloud.

"She'll be smiling down today." McKenzie nodded. "She wrote 'Whitlock' hoping to save her husband's life, and keep the memory of their love alive, if he failed to make it back. But she also encoded within it the treasonous acts of his best friend. Little did she know the lengths to which Quentin Hugh-Wynstanley would go to save his fortune and his reputation, and probably his life."

"Do you think he killed them both?"

"I suspect him of killing David. But, Rosemary? I don't know."

"An exhumation might answer that question?" Dalgleish shrugged.

"Yes, it might. But getting one agreed after all this time would be a battle all by itself."

"Aye..." Graham conceded. "Maybe one day, eh?"

"Maybe."

The team stood in silence for a moment, each contemplating the strange irony that Rosemary's coded messages, intended as protection from harm, had instead sparked a deadly chase that spanned generations.

"She had good intentions," McKenzie mused aloud, his gaze drifting back to the book. "But let's hope we've done what she wasn't able to. We've ended the cycle."

"Are we heading back, then?" Susan Robertson checked her watch. "The West Yorkshire lads are going to take the brothers to custody at their gaff, and they'll arrange transport to get him up to ours. They'll face charges here as well as in Edinburgh."

"Aye, those boys will have more interviews over the next

few days than they can shake a stick at. They are both facing multiple life sentences. My only regret is their father will probably go into a care home, and his estate broken up."

"I feel sorry for their father," Dalgleish pulled a face. "But not for the estate. Seems to me it was built on blood money. If it is broken up, it's probably just as well."

"Aye, you're probably right." McKenzie nodded. "Right, let's wrap it up here and get back. There are reports to write, statements to do, and I'm sure more than one of us is dreaming of a hot meal and a warm bed a little earlier tonight."

GRANT SAT FINISHING his report in the MIT office in Leith Police Station. The drone of distant conversations and the occasional ring of a telephone went unnoticed as he concentrated on getting the chronology right. When he finished, he leaned back in his chair, fingers steepled beneath his chin, eyes unfocused as they rested on the wall.

"Och, what are you doing daydreaming? I need that report." DCI Rob Sinclair strode over to his desk, looking at his watch. "You promised you'd have it in to me half an hour ago."

The DI came to with a crunch. "It's finished, sir. I was about to bring it in."

"Aye, you looked like you were, right enough."

"Sorry, Rob. I couldn't help thinking about everything that happened."

"You mean the murders?"

"Aye, those and any that might have gone unrecognised."

Sinclair frowned. "What do you mean?"

"Quentin Hugh-Wynstanley was a spy. Or, at least, he was part of a long-running spy ring, making money from selling secrets to enemies. God only knows how long it had been going on before him, but it didn't stop at the First World War. It continued at least until the end of the Second World War. They were going under the guise of a local Edinburgh history society. They were meeting at a book-shop in the Old Town. Had their own insignia and every-thing. And, all the while, they were passing secrets. Quentin Hugh-Wynstanley was still at it in the forties. That's why a prominent Nazi, Dieter Schmidt, was photographed with Quentin Hugh-Wynstanley and his chums. Stella Macleod knew. She had worked it out. She was going to tell me the day she was murdered."

"And you think there were more murders committed by this group during the wars?" Sinclair frowned.

"Aye. I think Quentin murdered Rosemary Whitlock's husband, David, his former best friend. And, maybe, even Rosemary herself? Perhaps she didn't pine away after all. If she suspected Hugh-Wynstanley of killing her husband, she may have confronted him. And I doubt he would have thought twice about taking her out as well. And, the worst of it, he never faced punishment for any of it. He just carried on selling secrets right through, until at least the end of the Second World War, according to Stella's notes. And, given that the spy ring's insignia was carved next to Lachlan Campbell's body, I suspect the Hugh-Wynstanley heirs were still at it. The insignia was a warning to those in the know to keep their mouths shut."

"Sounds to me like we'll be sending copies of your report up to British Intelligence? Let them do a thorough investigation of the goings on of this group?"

"Aye, sir. I'll leave all that to you."

Sinclair nodded. "Fair enough. But I'll need you available to answer questions if they need to know more."

"No problem. Dalgleish and I were wondering if we'd get permission to exhume Rosemary Whitlock, and have forensics run some tests on the remains. Check for poisons, maybe. Her death certificate said pneumonia, but I wonder how much influence Quentin might have had over that verdict."

"Exhume a famous writer?" Sinclair pulled a face.

"Aye, if he murdered her, she deserves justice. He stole her book while she lay dying. Perhaps that was no coincidence."

"I think exhuming her now might be a step too far. But, who knows, the intelligence services might agree with you, and maybe they'll pay for it."

McKenzie sighed. "Justice shouldn't depend on budgets."

"Aye, but we live in reality, don't we?" The DCI checked his watch. "Now, can I have that report? I've got to give the press conference later, and I need to know what I'm saying."

Grant lifted it from the desk. "Ach, here, it's all yours."

Helen approached the DI's desk as the DCI was about to leave. "Good news, sir. We have confirmation from West Yorkshire that the samples of paint we sent them from Fergus Murray's bike, match paint deposited on the bumper of the Hugh-Wynstanley's silver BMW. One or both of them knocked him off his bike."

Grant's eyes lit up. "That's great news... Thank you, Helen. I was worried the buggers would get away with that one."

"Aye, so was I." She nodded. "We're hoping to match the blonde hairs found in Stella's office, too. The brothers deny ever visiting her. If the hairs match, they'll be stuffed. They kept the murder scene clean, but they must have been pretty stressed when they tore her place up. One of them probably ran a hand through his hair."

"Good work, Helen. Keep me informed." McKenzie rose from his desk. "I'll join you and the others for a swift brew."

22

WAR-TORN

S he stood before him; her round dark-brown eyes searching his, as though hoping to read something else in their grey depths.

He knew this, and his heart sank again. This was the hardest thing he had ever had to do. And she looked even more beautiful, gazing up at him in that cool linen dress that made room for her ballooning mid-riff.

David Whitlock's hand trembled as he pushed stray brunette tendrils from the young nurse's heart-shaped face. "Yvette," he began, searching for the right words, his eyes moving to her hands as he took hold of them. Hers trembled as much as his. "I fell in love with you. Please, never doubt that. Whatever else you may feel or think about me, never doubt that I loved you. And I will also love the child you bear. This war has made a wasteland of countries and lives. And little of it makes sense. But, I love my wife. And I know she is waiting for me. I feel a heel for what I have done to her, and to you, and I hope one day you can forgive me. Please believe that you will always have a special place in my heart, and so too our child." He paused, lifting his eyes to the canvas tent that served as their temporary refuge, the fabric too thin to hold back an early November chill. Candles flickered, sending myriad shadows dancing around them.

The young woman lifted her tired eyes once again to his. She spoke in faltering English, delivered in the melodic French accent he adored. "I won't forget you. How could I? I will make sure our son knows his father loved him. She is so lucky... your wife... She must be a very special person-"

He stopped her there. "You are both special to me, and this makes it all the harder. We did not mean to fall in love. Had we met in peacetime, perhaps things would have been different. We would have admired each other from afar, without ever crossing the line. But war makes everything urgent. Not knowing if you will live, or how long you have left, it changes us. But believe me when I say that my only regret is hurting you. And I know I am hurting you. As brave as you are, I can see the pain in your eyes. I never wanted to be responsible for that. I'm a cad of the worst kind, I know, but I will never regret loving you. My actions were selfish, and for them I am deeply sorry. I implore you to accept money, which I will send you each month, to ensure our child's needs are met."

David fought against the sting of unshed tears. "I must try to right what wrongs I can from afar. When I am returned to Rosemary's side, this will be all I have to give."

Yvette nodded, fighting back tears, her hands rubbing her stomach. "Do you think you will ever get to see him?"

He sighed, closing his eyes; lifting his head before opening them again and returning his gaze back to hers. "I don't know. Maybe one day, when he is older-" He choked; the tears he had fought so hard to hold back fell like stones down his cheeks.

The young woman used her thumbs to wipe them away. "I have to go now. And you must put these things out of your head. Concentrate only on not getting killed out there. Stay alive for me... For us," she said, hands once more on her burgeoning belly.

"He will meet you one day, I hope. Don't forget us," she said, finally turning for the door.

"Wait," he called, reaching for her. He held the mother of his child for several minutes, his forehead resting on hers.

Finally, he kissed it. "Goodbye, Yvette. I will hold you in my heart."

~

THE BATTLEFIELD LAY EERILY SILENT, a stark contrast to the booming gunfire and agonised cries that had once filled its scorched and blackened air.

In their officers' quarters, Quentin Hugh-Wynstanley stood before David Whitlock, tie knot perfectly aligned; uniform pressed and unsullied. His expression was a stony mask, betraying no hint of their former friendship. "Tell Rosemary to destroy the book."

David, also in uniform, but in his shirt sleeves and braces, tie loose, and top button undone, sighed, shaking his head. "I'm afraid I can't do that. She worked so hard on it. It's not my place."

Quentin scowled. "You know what it contains... And what will happen to me and the rest of my group when someone else works it out, and they will. I thought we were friends."

"We were until you betrayed us. What were you thinking? Was it only ever about the money? What about honour, and pride, and love for one's country? What about those things? Do they not matter anymore? What have we been fighting and dying for? I have seen better men than you killed; their insides spilled on fields of mud and blood. And for what? So that you and your chums could deliver us to the enemy? You were my friend, but I no longer know who you are. If you cease all such activity, I will not report you, myself. But as for my wife's book? Let it be a reminder to never step out of line like that again. I wouldn't want *to be you on judgement day. Lord knows, I have done things for which I am sorry... It is the only reason I am not reporting you now, but I have never... and would never betray my country, or the men who risk their lives... Men that I now call friends. I do not recognise you, Quentin Hugh-Wynstanley. You have sullied your family's name and our friendship. Leave me now. I don't want to hit you. The guns have fallen silent. Peace is declared. You have a family to return to. Do so and never commit such treachery again." David Whitlock turned his back on his former friend.*

"Peace?" Quentin sneered, the word dripping bitterness. "There is no peace for men like us. You wouldn't understand; it was never about the betrayal. You and I have different beliefs. We adhere to different ideologies. And, if I made a little money along the way, what of it? The Brits still won, didn't they? No harm done? But your wife's book could change all that for me. I don't want it hanging over my head like the proverbial Damocles sword. The book is a map to my undoing, and I want it gone."

"You want it gone? Just like that? Because that would put things right, would it? If the book is gone, you are no longer a traitor, and I know longer know what you did. Is that it? You are the devil!" David declared, swinging back around. His eyes widened when he saw Quentin holding his pistol.

"Forgive me, David, but I cannot let you live," his former friend asserted, hand unnervingly still as he raised the weapon.

"Quentin, wait!"

A gunshot tore through the stillness, reverberating across the deserted battlefield. The few remaining birds scattered in the air. David Whitlock fell, eyes wide; blood seeping into the soil, joining that of so many others who had perished. One hour after the warring sides had declared peace, dark forces claimed yet another soul.

23

A FITTING END

A cool breeze shook the verdant branches of the surrounding trees as DI Grant McKenzie approached the prearranged final rendezvous with Pierre Fontaine in Princess Gardens, before the Frenchman left Edinburgh for his home country. He walked along the path until he saw the bench through a dwindling mist. It was empty.

"Sorry, I am late." Pierre came from behind, walking towards him; holding out his hand. "I'm taking an earlier flight back to Normandy tomorrow. I have been packing and tying up loose ends, But I wanted to say goodbye, and to thank you."

McKenzie accepted the handshake. "I should thank you," he said.

"Then we are thanking each other." Fontaine pushed his hands into his jacket pockets and smiled, though his eyes were soulful. He cleared his throat, taking a seat on the bench. "I was supposed to return Rosemary's book to Lachie today, before I returned to France. I was so impressed that he was willing to lend it to me."

"Under the circumstances, I think Lachlan would have wanted you to keep it." McKenzie sat next to the Frenchman. "We will release it soon. My intention is to have it sent to your home address, for you to do with it as you see fit."

Pierre raised both brows. "Really? You mean that? What about Rosemary's family? And your national archives? Won't they want it?"

"Perhaps, but you could loan it to them, or have copies made for the archives. Rosemary wrote that book to commemorate David and his family, knowing he could be killed in France. She believed he was the last of his male line. The final Whitlock. A military man from a long line of military men. She wanted his memory to live on and encoded within that book the names and meeting dates of a faux history society which had been passing secrets for money for decades. She did it to protect your great-great-grandfather from his best friend, Quentin, who had been one of those traitors. David died in Normandy, almost certainly killed by his former friend, and his letters from Rosemary and Yvette were taken. You are the descendant of David. It was your male line Rosemary described in her book. Your history. I think you should keep it. Finish reading it, at least."

Fontaine nodded. "Yvette named David's son David, after his father. His eldest son, my grandfather, was called Jacques, and my father is Clement."

"Will your father read the book?"

"I think he would. I will tell him about it, and we'll see..."

"I also wanted to give you these." Grant pulled a small bunch of letters from his overcoat pocket. "They are letters written by Yvette to David, and from Rosemary to David. We have taken copies of those needed for evidence. They are now returned to you."

Pierre accepted the pile, running his fingers over the faded handwriting on the top envelope.

"He was a good man, your great-great-grandfather. Flawed, but then aren't we all? We had to read many of the letters, I'm afraid, as part of this investigation. A necessary invasion of privacy... I could see how much Rosemary and Yvette loved him. They could not have cared for him as much if he wasn't a good man."

"I shall treasure these." Fontaine placed them in his jacket pocket. "Thank you."

"You're welcome." McKenzie shifted forward on the bench, about to stand.

"She found him, you know... Yvette..."

"Sorry?"

"She found him... After the war. They recovered his body."

"David Whitlock?"

"Yes. He is buried in a cemetery in Arras."

"But how?"

"She knew he must be dead. He had promised to write and send her money for the child. When neither arrived, Yvette was sure he had been killed. She believed so absolutely he would not have let her down that she began searching for him. Every time they found remains, she would go along to see them. Then, one day, around twelve years after the war, they found him. She recognised the neck chain and signet ring she had given to him. His uniform and papers were missing. I think Quentin had taken and destroyed them after David's murder. Clearing didn't know who the unknown man was. But Yvette knew. She told them he was her husband and arranged for him to be buried in

Arras. She buried him under the name David Fontaine. I will change all that, I promise, and give him his rightful name back. I will see that he has a suitable epitaph, one befitting the hero he was."

"You knew about him all along, didn't you?" The DI pressed his lips together.

"I did. But, as I told you, at the time you interviewed me, I was still terrified of being blamed for Lachlan Campbell's death. I had Rosemary's book. I didn't think you would believe my explanation."

"You should have been honest with us."

"Yes, I see that now. I also knew of the symbol, and the society. Lachlan mentioned it to me, but he didn't go into detail. Perhaps he didn't know everything at that stage. But he was doing a lot of research and writing notes. He told me he was looking into something big, and would continue once he had the book back." He shuddered. "Sometimes I wonder if I should give the book to the archives. Death seems to have followed it around."

McKenzie shook his head. "Death followed the Hugh-Wynstanleys around. The book didn't kill people... But members of that family did. I almost felt sorry for Horatio and William. They were born into the mess. But they could have chosen a different path, so I don't feel bad for them now."

Fontaine nodded. "Yes, I guess you are right... The book was never the problem." His gaze shifted to the early morning sun filtering through the trees, casting twisted shadows across the damp grass. "Lachlan said they called themselves The Keepers, calling themselves the protectors of secret knowledge."

"Ha..." The DI tutted, shaking his head. "Of course they did. But it wasn't knowledge or history they were protecting, was it? It was themselves, and the fortune they were making selling their country downriver."

"David didn't know he had made friends with a monster."

"Aye, exactly."

Fontaine continued. "And when Lachie was found dead, I thought I might be next."

"Lachlan didn't tell them you had the book, did he?"

"They told me, while I was a captive in their house, they wanted the book back. You see, they sold it at a secret auction, believing no-one would understand its true significance. After he bought it, they called Lachlan, 'the old man', and they told me they had believed him a simple collector. But he began working things out, and spoke to Stella, and posted on social media that he was onto something. He deleted the post too late. The brothers had seen it. They went after Lachlan, but he wouldn't tell them where the book was. I feel like he died protecting me."

The DI shook his head. "Don't blame yourself, they would have killed him, anyway. They didn't want him working it all out and telling the authorities. Their family's reputation and fortune were on the line." He held out his hand. "Well, Monsieur Fontaine, I wish you all the very best for the future. We will be in touch again if necessary but, otherwise, I'll say goodbye."

They shook hands once more.

"If Rosemary had met you, she would have approved. Read her book, Pierre. I know she would have liked that."

"I will." Fontaine nodded. "Goodbye, Inspector. And thank you. Again."

McKenzie watched him walk away, pondering what the Frenchman had said about David's body being found all those years ago. It would have been too late for Rosemary.

She had already passed. Perhaps that was why Yvette kept him in Arras, close to herself and her son.

The DI gave himself a mental shake. He had work to do, and there were other cases pending. He set off back to his car.

IN THE CANTEEN of a Northern England prison, the Hugh-Wynstanley brothers ate their food in silence. Gone were the tailored suits and the confidence they were untouchable. Now, their eyes shifted this way and that, wary of those around, afraid of the beefed-up brutes covered in tattoos who glared at them from the tables opposite.

The clatter of trays and the grating of chair legs against polished floors echoed in the air. The stench of overcooked cabbage and stewed chicken invaded their nostrils, a far cry from their once indulgent diet of fine wines and pheasant from the estate.

They watched as, one by one, most of the inmates filed out of the hall.

"We have to get out of here, they'll kill us." William said, his worried gaze wandering the room.

Horatio dropped his fork onto the tray with a clatter. His gaze settling on a trio of thugs across the room. The men huddled in a corner, muscles straining the fabric of poorly fitting prison uniforms. They turned to stare at the brothers, their expressions a warning. A message.

The Hugh-Wynstanleys hunched over their half-eaten food.

William leaned closer to his brother. "You'd better think of something," he murmured, clutching a spoon so tightly his knuckles turned white.

"Quiet, Will." Horatio scowled at his brother's panic-stricken face. "Keep your voice down. Do you want to give them an excuse to come over?"

"Don't you have any plan at all?" William's voice lowered to a whisper, gaze darting from the prisoners, to the guards, and the exit doors. "We're sitting ducks. If we don't find a way out, they will find a way to get to us."

Horatio cut him off. "You think I'm not working on it?"

With fear in the younger Hugh-Wynstanley's eyes, and frustration in the elder brother's, they awaited their fate in the grimy confines of the place that would be their home for the next several decades.

THE END

AFTERWORD

Watch out for Book 4 in the DI McKenzie Series, coming soon...

Mailing list: You can join my emailing list here : AnnamarieMorgan.com

Facebook page: AnnamarieMorganAuthor

Book 1: Murder on Arthur's Seat

When DI Grant McKenzie's world is thrown into chaos by the sudden disappearance of his twenty-one-year-old nephew, he is determined to uncover the truth no matter the cost.

As he and his team are plunged into a dark and sinister web of organised crime, McKenzie must face a wealthy and elusive kingpin who believes himself untouchable. With the fate of his nephew hanging in the balance, McKenzie and his team will stop at nothing to bring the criminal mastermind to justice.

Book 2: Murder at Greyfriars Kirk

When a young influencer is found dead in an Edinburgh

graveyard, the contents of her last video provide an enigmatic, if not downright cryptic, insight into the woman's last moments.

DI Grant McKenzie cannot shake the feeling the woman was trying to communicate more than a historical tale for her followers. Did she know what was about to happen?

As more influencers fall prey to the same killer, the DI and his team face a heart-stopping race to find an evil psychopath who sneaks up on preoccupied prey; the man the press has named The Gimbal Killer.

You might also like to read the author's other books.

The DI Giles Series:

Book 1: Death Master:

After months of mental and physical therapy, Yvonne Giles, an Oxford DI, is back at work and that's just how she likes it. So when she's asked to hunt the serial killer responsible for taking apart young women, the DI jumps at the chance but hides the fact she is suffering debilitating flashbacks. She is told to work with Tasha Phillips, an in-her-face, criminal psychologist. The DI is not enamoured with the idea. Tasha has a lot to prove. Yvonne has a lot to get over. A tentative link with a 20 year-old cold case brings them closer to the truth but events then take a horrifyingly personal turn.

Book 2: You Will Die

After apprehending an Oxford Serial Killer, and almost losing her life in the process, DI Yvonne Giles has left England for a quieter life in rural Wales.Her peace is shattered when she is asked to hunt a priest-killing psychopath, who taunts the police with messages inscribed on the corpses.Yvonne requests the help of Dr. Tasha Phillips, a psychologist and friend, to aid in the hunt. But the killer is one step ahead and the ultimatum, he sets them, could leave everyone devastated.

Book 3: Total Wipeout

A whole family is wiped out with a shotgun. At first glance, it's an open-and-shut case. The dad did it, then killed himself. The deaths follow at least two similar family wipeouts – attributed to the financial crash.

So why doesn't that sit right with Detective Inspector Yvonne Giles? And why has a rape occurred in the area, in the weeks preceding each family's demise? Her seniors do not believe there are questions to answer. DI Giles must therefore risk everything, in a high-stakes investigation of a mysterious masonic ring and players in high finance.

Can she find the answers, before the next innocent family is wiped out?

Book 4: Deep Cut

In a tiny hamlet in North Wales, a female recruit is murdered whilst on Christmas home leave. Detective Inspector Yvonne Giles is asked to cut short her own leave, to investigate. Why was the young soldier killed? And is her death related to several alleged suicides at her army base? DI Giles this it is, and that someone powerful has a dark secret they will do anything to hide.

Book 5: The Pusher

Young men are turning up dead on the banks of the River Severn. Some of them have been missing for days or even weeks. The only thing the police can be sure of, is that the men have drowned. Rumours abound that a mythical serial killer has turned his attention from the Manchester canal to the waterways of Mid-Wales. And now one of CID's own is missing. A brand new recruit with everything to live for. DI Giles must find him before it's too late.

Book 6: Gone

Children are going missing. They are not heard from again until sinister requests for cryptocurrency go viral. The public must pay or the children die. For lead detective Yvonne Giles, the case is complicated enough. And then the unthinkable happens...

Book 7: Bone Dancer

A serial killer is murdering women, threading their bones back together, and leaving them for police to find. Detective Inspector Yvonne Giles must find him before more innocent victims die. Problem is, the killer wants her and will do anything he can to get her. Unaware that she, herself, is is a target, DI Giles risks everything to catch him.

Book 8: Blood Lost

A young man comes home to find his whole family missing. Half-eaten breakfasts and blood spatter on the lounge wall are the only clues to what happened...

Book 9: Angel of Death

The peace of the Mid-Wales countryside is shattered, when a female eco-warrior is found crucified in a public wood. At first, it would appear a simple case of finding which of the woman's enemies had had her killed. But DI Yvonne Giles has no idea how bad things are going to get. As the body count rises, she will need all of her instincts, and the skills of those closest to her, to stop the murderous rampage of the Angel of Death.

Book 10: Death in the Air

Several fatal air collisions have occurred within a few months in rural Wales. According to the local Air Accidents Investigation Branch (AAIB) inspector, it's a coincidence. Clusters happen. Except, this cluster is different. DI Yvonne Giles suspects it when she hears some of the witness statements but, when an AAIB inspector is found dead under a bridge, she knows it.

Something is way off. Yvonne is determined to get to the bottom of the mystery, but exactly how far down the treacherous rabbit hole is she prepared to go?

Book 11: Death in the Mist

The morning after a viscous sea-mist covers the seaside town of Aberystwyth, a young student lies brutalised within one hundred yards of the castle ruins.

DI Yvonne Giles' reputation precedes her. Having successfully captured more serial killers than some detectives have caught colds, she is seconded to head the murder investigation team, and hunt down the young woman's killer.

What she doesn't know, is this is only the beginning...

Book 12: Death under Hypnosis

When the secretive and mysterious Sheila Winters approaches Yvonne Giles and tells her that she murdered someone thirty years before, she has the DI's immediate attention.

Things get even more strange when Sheila states:
She doesn't know who.

She doesn't know where.

She doesn't know why.

Book 13: Fatal Turn

A seasoned hiker goes missing from the Dolfor Moors after recording a social media video describing a narrow cave he intends to explore. A tragic accident? Nothing to see here, until a team of cavers disappear on a coastal potholing expedition, setting off a string of events that has DI Giles tearing her hair out. What, or who is the thread that ties this series of disappearances together?

A serial killer, thriller murder-mystery set in Wales.

Book 14: The Edinburgh Murders

A newly-retired detective from the Met is murdered in a murky alley in Edinburgh, a sinister calling card left with the body.

The dead man had been a close friend of psychologist Tasha Phillips, giving her her first gig with the Met decades before.

Tasha begs DI Yvonne Giles to aid the Scottish police in solving the case.

In unfamiliar territory, and with a ruthless killer haunting the streets, the DI plunges herself into one of the darkest, most terrifying cases of her career. Who exactly is The Poet?

Book 15: A Picture of Murder

Men are being thrown to their deaths in rural Wales.

At first glance, the murders appear unconnected until DI Giles uncovers potential links with a cold case from the turn of the Millennium.

Someone is eliminating the witnesses to a double murder.

DI Giles and her team must find the perpetrator before all the witnesses are dead.

Book 16: The Wilderness Murders

People are disappearing from remote locations.

Abandoned cars, neatly piled belongings, and bizarre last photographs, are the only clues for what happened to them.

Did they run away? Or, as DI Giles suspects, have they fallen prey to a serial killer who is taunting police with the heinous pieces of a puzzle they must solve if they are to stop the wilderness murderer.

Book 17: The Bunker Murders

A murder victim found in a shallow grave has DI Yvonne Giles and her team on the hunt for both the killer and a motive for the well-loved man's demise.

Yvonne cannot help feeling the killing is linked to a string of female disappearances stretching back nearly two decades.

Someone has all the answers, and the DI will stop at nothing to find them and get to the bottom of this perplexing mystery.

Book 18: The Garthmyl Murders

A missing brother and friends with dark secrets have DI Giles turning circles after a body is found face-down in the pond of a local landmark.

Stymied by a wall of silence and superstition, Yvonne and her team must dig deeper than ever if they are to crack this impossible case.

Who, or what, is responsible for the Garthmyl murders?

Book 19: The Signature

When a young woman is found dead inside a rubbish dumpster after a night out, police chiefs are quick to label it a tragic accident. But as more bodies surface, Detective Inspector Yvonne Giles is convinced a cold-blooded murderer is on the loose. She believes the perpetrator is devious and elusive, disabling CCTV cameras in the area, and leaving them with little to go on. With time running out, Giles and her team must race against the clock to catch the killer or killers before they strike again.

Book 20: The Incendiary Murders

When the Powys mansion belonging to an ageing rock star is rocked by a deadly explosion, Detective Inspector Yvonne Giles finds herself tasked with a case of murder, suspicion, and secrets. As shockwaves ripple through the community, Giles must pierce the impenetrable facades of the characters surrounding the case, racing the clock to find the culprit and prevent further bombings. With an investigation full of twists and turns, DI Yvonne Giles must unravel the truth before it's too late.

Book 21 - The Park Murders

When two people are left dead and four others are seriously ill in hospital after a visit to a local nature park in rural Wales, DI Giles and her team find themselves in a race against time to stop a killer or killers hell-bent on terrorising the community. As the investigation deepens, the team must draw on all of their skill and experience to hunt down the elusive Powys poisoner before more lives are lost.

Book 22 - The Powys Murders

Three bodies are discovered in a wood when snow and ice melt from the Powys countryside. Police suspect the dead men were involved in a road traffic collision before they ran off into the darkness and succumbed to exposure.

What made them run uphill into the wilderness instead of downhill to the nearest town? Were all of their injuries inflicted by the collision? Or something more sinister? And why was one victim missing his shoes?

DI Yvonne Giles suspects foul play, believing the men ran the wrong way because they were terrified. Who, or what, was responsible for the deaths of The Powys Three? And are others at risk from the same evil?

Remember to watch out for Book 23 in the DI Giles Series, coming soon...

Printed in Great Britain
by Amazon

43697458R00108